Holiday Date

By Debbie Ioanna

Copyright © Debbie Ioanna 2020

ISBN: 9798619542554

Debbie Ioanna has asserted her rights to be identified as the author of this work.

All rights reserved. This book or any portion thereof may not be reproduced or used in any manner whatsoever without the express written permission of the publisher, except for the use of brief quotations in a book review.

This book is a work of fiction. Names, characters, places and incidents are either a product of the author's imagination or are used fictitiously.

Indie Author and blogger, Debbie Ioanna, brings you the second instalment of the 'Blind Date' series.

'*Blind Date*' is available to buy on Amazon.

Also by the author

Abberton House

The Runaway Girl

Contents

Chapter 1	1
Chapter 2	4
Chapter 3	16
Chapter 4	20
Chapter 5	24
Chapter 6	31
Chapter 7	41
Chapter 8	50
Chapter 9	57
Chapter 10	60
Chapter 11	66
Chapter 12	71
Chapter 13	79
Chapter 14	82
Chapter 15	93
Chapter 16	101
Chapter 17	106
Chapter 18	109
Chapter 19	114
Chapter 20	120
Chapter 21	125
Chapter 22	130
Chapter 23	136
Chapter 24	139
Chapter 25	143
Chapter 26	152
Chapter 27	159
Chapter 28	163
Chapter 29	171
Chapter 30	179
Chapter 31	182
Bonus	189

ACKNOWLEDGMENTS

For my cat Cleo, who has never been acknowledged, even though she was the inspiration for our loveable Bing :) I love you, kitty. Sorry about bringing a baby into the house... I know you hate small people.

1

My legs straddled Zack's naked body as he was handcuffed to my bed, totally at my mercy. The cuffs dug into his wrists as he struggled between pain and pleasure.

"Do you want me to stop?" I asked over his cries of passion as I kissed his chest, working my way down his body. His body trembling under mine.

"No," Zack cried out. "Oh, baby, no, keep doing that."

As I finally gave into his body's demands, I climbed on top of him and we began to move together, quickly. The headboard banged against the wall, making the bed vibrate beneath us.

"Jenny..." He called out, loudly.

"Yeah," I said, feeling my orgasm about to rip through me as he said my name. "Oh, yeah."

The room seemed to shake as the bed bounced harder and harder.

"Jenny!" He said louder, but less like he was enjoying himself.

"Yeah?" I asked.

"Jenny!" He shouted, with a more feminine voice…

"Jenny!?" Sarah's voice bellowed at me. "For god's sake, will you wake up? The plane has landed."

Feeling flushed, I surveyed my surroundings. Other passengers were crowding the aisles getting their coats and bags from the overhead storage as the stewardesses looked on in frustration. People were always in a rush once the plane landed to grab their things, but I never could understand why. It's not like our luggage is going to be waiting for us as soon as we exit. I can guarantee it'll be another hour before we leave the airport.

"How long was I snoozing?" I asked Sarah, rubbing my eyes and hoping I wasn't making sex noises in my sleep.

"I'm not sure, a while. How can you even sleep on a plane? It's so uncomfortable." She rubbed her neck. "And how on earth did you manage to sleep through a plane landing? That's just bizarre."

"Just naturally gifted at being able to sleep anywhere," I laughed, stretching out my arms. I didn't want to tell her I was exhausted because Zack and I had been up all the night before having wild sex to prepare for not seeing each other for nearly a whole week. We had not been apart for this long in the nine months we'd been together. "I can't wait to get up and stretch my legs. Three hours is a long time to sit still. I'm bursting for a wee."

"You could have just used the airplane loos you know. You didn't need to hold it in."

"I don't use airplane loos." I said, thinking back to the first time I attempted it. I had stared into the toilet, fearing I would be sucked out of the plane and plunge six miles to my death. Absolute nonsense of course, that wouldn't happen, but I did chicken out in the end. Instead, I just used some tissue to blow my nose and chucked it in the bowl, but when I flushed, I swear I felt a puff of air hit my face. Fears confirmed. I would have been sucked out of the toilet. So, from then on, no matter how much I needed it, I would never use an airplane toilet, nope.

We were finally allowed to leave the plane, so we followed the crowd through the airport, through the passport checks and then to pick up our luggage. Or rather, stand around for twenty-five minutes for the conveyor belt to be switched on, and then a further ten minutes for ours to appear. Once suitcases were collected, and stress levels reduced, we were finally able to start our girly holiday.

2

If it were possible to eat a smell, then I would be munching on the air right now. One nostril was overdosing on freshly ground coffee and the other was having a foodgasm from freshly cooked pizza dough. I had officially reached my own version of heaven.

    Sarah and I had just arrived at our hotel after a somewhat terrifying taxi ride from the airport. We should have just taken the train like every other well-educated tourist, but we thought it would be much more luxurious to have our own chariot. There were to be no expenses spared on this holiday. Seeing as though this June weekend should have been Sarah's wedding to Max The Wanker, we decided to splash out over the next few days so the month of June will never need to be tainted by heart-breaking memories. We had a full plan for this gal-tastic break. Sarah would have a wonderful time, even if it killed me. Judging from previous holiday experiences with Sarah, I'm not exaggerating.

    We were staying at a small, family run hotel on the edge of Rome. The elderly owner, Leonardo, was approximately four-foot-tall and the cutest little Italian man I had ever met. He had a permanent smile on his olive-skinned face. His shiny, bald head reflected the sun and it did not seem to matter how hot it was today, he wore a clean white shirt buttoned to the top and a silver tie which was pinned to his shirt. I wanted to adopt him. His wife, Maria, was just as tiny as her husband but as terrifying as a tiger that hadn't eaten for days. She was like a yappy Yorkshire Terrier snapping at your feet. A floral scarf was hiding her hair and she wore a matching apron, making her look like the Italian equivalent of Nora Batty. She handed us biscotti as we arrived which we felt obligated to eat in front of her, fearing we would be scolded if we refused.

"Mmmm," I said as I tried to crunch down on the hard biscuit without breaking my teeth, "delicious." I wonder if my travel insurance would cover dental emergencies.

"Si, delizioso!" she barked before muttering something in Italian to her husband and walking heavy-footed through another door. We all jumped as we heard the biscotti tray bang down on a worktop.

"My wife, ah," Leonardo began. I loved his accent. "She will bring coffee to your room, so you can settle." He smiled, as though he was the most content man on earth.

"Oh, that sounds great," Sarah said, "but we really want to go straight back out to explore."

"Yeah, it's still only early so we thought we'd go for a wander before dinner."

"Ah, wonder?" he looked confused.

"A wander, you know, like a walk around, to see what is nearby."

"Ah, ok, si si. Here, your key." He handed us an old, rustic key with a tag showing the number '4' dangling on very fragile piece of string. "Up a-the stair, left," he gestured, "your room at end of corridor."

"Thank you!" We both smiled, but Leonardo looked worried.

"I ah, I go tell Maria we no need coffee."

He anxiously shuffled down to the door Maria went through and I suddenly felt very guilty.

"Do you think she'll go mad?" I asked Sarah. "I feel awful."

"If he's made it to a hundred years old and she's not killed him yet then I think he'll be ok. Come on, let's get these bags away so we can go back out into the sun."

Sarah and I grabbed our things and headed up the stairs, following Leonardo's directions. The carpet looked as old as Leonardo and his wife, the walls looked aged and the ceiling paint was peeling off, but somehow it did not matter. It looked chic, as though it was intentionally decorated that way. Unlike the peeling paint in my own bathroom that I keep putting off fixing. DIY is not my forte.

We unlocked our door and walked into our room which would be our home for the next few nights. We were not disappointed. The air conditioning in particular was a welcome treat. The floor tiles were a deep orange colour, very Mediterranean. There were two single beds covered in clean white bedding with mustard yellow cushions and throws, and the curtains hanging in the windows matched it all nicely. It was all very modern. I was expecting dull colours and net curtains but clearly Maria had sense to bring in a professional decorator. Each bedside table had its own lamp as well as a vase with fresh flowers on one and the bible on the other. (Sorry, God, but I've brought *Twilight* instead. Maybe next time).

The tall window turned out to be a glass door leading to a small balcony, just big enough for a small round table and two chairs. It would be a squeeze to get us both out there without fear of being pushed over the railings, but I'm sure we would manage whilst sober.

In the corner of the room was a two-seater sofa with a black metal coffee table in front of it. I spotted a plate on top with yet more biscotti, (Maria has been busy) and a small laminated note was propped up against an ice bucket which was busy chilling a bottle of prosecco.

Sarah picked up the note and read it out in her best attempt at an Italian accent.

"Welcome dear guests to La Casa di Angelo

We hope you enjoy your stay with us and your time in Rome

Breakfast will be brought to your room at 7:30 which can be eaten on balcony

Ask for Leonardo if have any problem

Grazie"

"Perfecto," Sarah smiled, resuming her normal Yorkshire accent. "Breakfast in bed." She put the note back on the table and opened the door to the balcony and stepped out.

"I'm just going to use the loo," I lied. "I'll be back in a tick."

I had switched my phone on at the airport but it had not connected to the local network when we were there. I had promised Sarah a phone free holiday, but I had to check on both of my boyfriends.

There it was, a WhatsApp message waiting for me with a photo of my two favourite men. The one that cuddles me at night, keeps me warm and makes me feel needed. And the other, the sex god boyfriend of mine that I just can't get enough of. Ok, yes, he cuddles me at night too, but on the rare nights we are not together, I have Bing to keep me company.

"Hope you've arrived baby," Zack said in his message, "we miss you already xxxx"

In the photo, Zack and Bing were laying on my couch. Bing was asleep on Zack's bare chest. Oh, what I wouldn't give to be there right now. I can't believe that I am jealous of my own cat. My dream from my airplane nap has left me feeling so horny... I hope Sarah doesn't catch me dry humping my pillow in my sleep.

"We're here! It's so hot!! Gorgeous though. Can't wait for pizza. I'll try not to come back the size of a whale :P Love you Xxxx"

Knock knock.

"Have you shat yourself?" Sarah called from the other side of the door. "Let me in, I need a wee."

I opened the door and she saw the phone in my hand.

"You don't need to hide your phone, you spoon. You're allowed to communicate with your fella."

She sat herself on the toilet and I finally had a look around the bathroom, running my hand along the bath.

"It's all marble," I observed. "Marble floor, tiles, bath, sink, everything."

"I know, it's gorgeous. Nice and cool in here too."

It was. There was no window and the air conditioning had been working very nicely in the whole room. I walked out of the bathroom and out to the balcony where the heat hit me. Our room faced another building, so there was not much of a view. It was a very narrow street so there was no breeze coming in through the door either, making it very humid.

In hot, humid weather, there are two types of girls. There are the girls who can wear their long hair free flowing and held back out of their eyes with their sunglasses on top of their head. They can also have a full face of makeup on without the risk of a sweaty upper lip. Sarah falls into this category of women. And then there are the other types of girls. The ones whose hair sticks to their sun-creamed shoulders so it needs to be tied back in a boring, unflattering ponytail. They can't wear foundation as it melts straight back off. Any attempt at eyeliner and they look like a member of the Addams family. Their upper lips sweat profusely and they can't walk around in skirts because their legs chafe. Unfortunately for me, I fall into this category of women.

"That's better." Sarah joined me on the balcony. "Where shall we go first? Shall we just go for a walk and then find somewhere to eat? I know you're dying for an authentic pizza cooked by actual Italians and not from the frozen food section at Tesco."

"I'm in Italy, this is my dream come true!" I said, fanning myself with a tissue I found in my pocket. "Pizza is top of my list of things to do. Sightseeing comes later. Pizza over Pisa."

"Well luckily for you, Pisa is in a different place entirely. Ok, let's freshen up and head out before Maria brings us more biscotti."

Back inside, I dug my little bag out of my suitcase and transferred over some necessities for walking around in a hot, foreign country: euros, tissues, compact mirror and my trusty handheld fan. Zack thought it was hilarious that I had a handheld fan, rather than a battery powered one like the rest of the modern world. Like a child, I got in a grump with him. I've had this fan for years and it has never let me down yet. As soon as he started nuzzling my neck though, I couldn't help but forgive him. Mock my fan? That's fine. Burn my house down? That's fine. Just keep doing what you're doing…

Once my flutters were under control, I brushed my hair back and made sure it was all tied up properly, including those annoying short bits of hair that always need pinning down to my head. As soon as they've managed to grow to a normal length, I seem to get another batch of short, useless fluff. Once they get even a little bit moist with sweat, they curl and sit on my forehead making me look like Dot Cotton.

I pulled out my sun cream and we both topped up, knowing the sneaky sun had a way of getting you, even if you spent most of the time in the shade.

Once we were ready, we headed out of the room and downstairs. There was a lot of banging and raised voices in the background. Well, we could make out Maria shouting. Poor Leonardo. Maybe I should just adopt him as my Nonno so I can take him home and look after him. Bing would love him.

We stepped out of the door, through what felt like a heat curtain, and out on to the cobbled street.

"So," Sarah said as soon as we were a safe distance from Maria's rage. "Where shall we go first?"

She had downloaded an app to her phone which was full of tourist information, locations and things to do. There was also a map which pinpointed our exact location. Her sunglasses were sat on the top of her head, holding her glossy hair back as she focused on the map. Not an ounce of sweat on her face. Cow.

"Wherever you like. It's only four o'clock so not time to eat yet." I pulled out my fan and started wafting myself, feeling the sweat creeping up on the back of my neck.

I was hoping she would suggest going for gelato or coffee and sitting outside a coffee shop. Something nice, easy, relaxed and in the shade. There was plenty of time to do tourist stuff, but for today it would be nice to stay near to the hotel and get used to the heat.

"Oo! Let's walk to the Coliseum! It's only a mile away!"

A mile, in this heat? I will have burned off my pizza before I've even eaten it if we walk over there. I hope I don't get grumpy. Heat and hunger can be a dangerous combination.

"Let's do it," I smiled, determined to make it an amazing holiday for her.

And so, we set off walking on the cobbles which were probably laid when Adam and Eve were stealing apples from the tree. Luckily, being from Halifax, we were used to cobbled roads trying to trip us up. I had no idea where we were going but I trusted Sarah's navigational skills, even if we were in a foreign country relying on a phone app.

"Have you seen this?" she asked. "Look at the walls."

They were old and looked like a strong gust of wind could blow them down however they had managed to survive this long. Some of the local authorities back home could learn a thing or two from our ancient Roman friends. Maybe the Romans could consider invading England again and fixing our roads. I might make a suggestion to the Pope.

"Yeah, very old." I was not sure how one was supposed to compliment a wall. Very bricky? Although these weren't bricks. They're made from old stone. Very stony? I have no idea how to entertain my history loving friend.

"No, you spoon, look!" This time she pointed. Carved into the wall was a cross. A crucifix. It was very worn, hard to see, but stood out once you spotted it. "I wonder if there is an old church nearby that we could look at."

"It's a very religious city. I'll bet there are more churches than coffee shops."

The sun was hitting my shoulders now and I was beginning to feel the burn, even through my factor thirty sun cream. I should have brought some with me for a quick top up.

"Will you show me your white bits when you get back?" Zack asked.

"There might be more red bits than white bits, but I'll see what I can do."

I can't let myself get burned on this trip. Burned skin is painful skin which turns to peeling skin. I don't want Zack treating me like a leper when I get home. This many days without his touch is an awful thought. I want to be able to jump on him as soon as I see him. He won't want me near him if I'm crumbling like a Cadbury flake.

We carried on with our walk and we knew we were heading to the centre of Rome as the further we walked, the busier the streets became. Suddenly, we were walking amongst a crowd of people. We had been warned by friends to keep our bags close to us and away from pickpockets which were rife in the city.

We decided to make a right down a quiet and narrow path for a bit of breathing space. There was a tall building to the right which had small shops on the ground floor and what must have been four floors of apartments above with shutters on all the windows. I was not sure what the old building on the left was though. Sarah had put her phone away now, for fear of it being snatched, so she wasn't too sure where we were either.

"I wonder what this old building is," Sarah said, but I didn't respond. After an hour of walking, I could feel myself getting grumpy. The heat. The sweat. The feel of hard stone beneath my flimsy sandals. I need to sit. I need a drink. I need food.

Sarah seemed to pick up on my deteriorating mood. Luckily, she knows how to handle such a tricky and delicate situation.

"Let's walk around to see what it is and then we can head for food."

It sounded like something you would say to a whining child to stop them from moaning, but it worked. We followed the path to the end of the road and rejoined the crowd, following them like sheep to the front of the building. And, wow. This was not just any old building.

The enormous roof was being held up by rows and rows of pillars. I couldn't make out the wording that was carved into the front, but it didn't stop me attempting to read it out loud. There were hundreds of folk stood in and around the pillars taking photos, touching them, leaning against them, sitting on the floor next to them. Those pesky Instagrammers were trying to get creative too. Yorkshire is filled with old buildings with impressive architecture and carvings, but this was something else.

"Well," Sarah began. "Wow."

That is all that needed to be said about the Pantheon. Wow.

3

"How much?" I exclaimed, loudly.

We had managed to pull ourselves away from the Pantheon and decided on a cheeky ice cream to cool us down before finding somewhere for tea. There was a gelato stand not far from there and I was busy reading the menu board.

"Why is it so expensive?"

"I don't know, but I'm not paying that much for a bottle of water," I said a little too loudly. "It's bloody mental!"

I figured that as we were in the capital city, things would be a little more expensive here. Just like when you head to London and the drinks cost a little more there, but this was taking the piss. It was going to cost nearly fifty euros for two bottles of water. I know we agreed not to skimp on this trip, but unless that water comes with flakes of gold floating in it, I'm not paying those kinds of prices, even if I was beginning to feel dehydrated.

"Come on, there must be a little shop or something around here where it is a lot cheaper."

"Mi scusi, ladies?" A deep voice said from behind us.

We turned to see who was talking to us. If they were even talking to us. There were so many people stood around us that we could have been mistaken. Then he stepped forward. I don't know how he was able to cope in his suit, but there was not an ounce of sweat on him. His long, black hair was swept back behind his ears and he had beautiful coloured skin. His hair was beautiful. *He* was beautiful.

"I'm so sorry, ladies," he said again in very good English. "Please, come."

He gestured for us to follow him, away from the crowd.

"Is it safe?" I asked Sarah, whose mouth was almost touching the floor.

"If he wants to kidnap me, he can. Come on."

She grabbed my hand and pulled me through the crowd to follow the mysterious Italian man. He did not lead us down an abandoned alley so there was no need to get Liam Neeson on speed dial. Instead, he just took us away from the hoard of people into a more open area near the Pantheon.

"I'm sorry, I know you are on holiday so I no bother you for long, but my advice? Don't buy from 'ere." He pointed to the gelato stand where we had just been, and to the other vendors scattered around. "You should buy from less busy place. Outside the main part of the city. Is cheaper. These prices? Crazy."

"Ah, right," I said. Sarah was in a trance listening to him speak. "Thank you. It's so nice of you to tell us. We'll find somewhere else."

"How long you been in Rome?" he asked.

"We only arrived this afternoon. We were just going to have a walk before finding somewhere to eat. Where would you recommend?"

"You will find lots of places hidden in the old roads. If there are tourists? Keep walking. If there are Italians? You know is a good place." He had a great smile.

"Thank you," Sarah finally woke up from her man-coma. "Are you from Rome?"

"No, I am from Foggia, a little bit south of 'ere. I now live in Rome, for work."

"Ah that sounds wonderful."

They seemed to be staring deeply into each other's eyes. A subtle smile, and the odd twinkle. All thoughts of Max The Wanker and the abandoned wedding had been pushed well out of Sarah's mind for now, thanks to our new Italian stallion friend.

"My name is Alessandro." He was out of his trance too and held out his hands to shake ours in return.

"I'm Sarah, and this is Jenny."

"It is nice to meet you ladies. But I must apologise. I must leave. Maybe we will see each other again, yes?"

"Yes. That would be great, yes. Jenny?" Sarah looked at me.

"Absolutely." This was the first time in a long time that any smile on her face had seemed genuine. Until now, any man who dared to speak to her was kindly told to eff off. "We're here for a few days so, definitely."

"Good, good." He fumbled around in his pocket and pulled out a card. "This is my number. We can meet for a drink, or something." I could almost feel the electricity as his hand touched Sarah's as she took the card from him. She ran her other hand through her hair, brushing a strand of it behind her ear. She wasn't even blushing. If that were me, I would be as red as a pepperoni.

"I'll let you know what we're doing and then we can arrange something."

"That sounds wonderful. Grazie." He stepped back, ready to walk away from us, having one final glance of Sarah. "Ciao, ladies."

"Yes, ciao."

4

"Did you hear how he said his name though?" Sarah had been obsessing over her new Italian friend throughout our entire meal. We followed Alessandro's advice and found a restaurant nearby our hotel that was filled with locals. And he was right. The food was perfecto as well as cheapo.

"I did." I picked up another slice of pizza. I was in full on foodgasm mode and hardly even listening to what she was saying.

"Alessandro. Oh, how his tongue rolled when he said it. Alessandrrro. Imagine what else that tongue could do."

"Well," I used my napkin to wipe melted cheese from my chin, "we're here for a little while longer. Plenty of time to find out. My god, this is good pizza."

"Do you think we should meet up with him? Is that a good idea? No, we can't. I can't."

"Why not?" I asked, taking another huge bite.

"Because it's our holiday. A girly holiday. Not a man meeting holiday."

"Neither was Zante in 2010, and we both know how that turned out."

"That was different! We were twenty-one. Single girls in their twenties can get away with that kind of stuff. I'm thirty-one now. It is time to be mature. Sensible. One must refrain from climbing on top of sexy Italian men."

"What are you talking about? You can do what you want. It's not just for girls in their twenties."

"Of course it is! Didn't you ever notice the looks we'd get when we were out from the older women? They hated us."

"Don't be daft, no one hated us."

"Of course they did! It's a known fact that single women in their thirties hate single women in their twenties. They're the threat. They're young, naïve, up for anything, boobs in the right place. Whereas us, we've mellowed, and our boobs need extra support."

I tried to ignore the giant, sparkly pink elephant in the room, but it was difficult. Max The Wanker's pregnant girlfriend, Ellie, was in her twenties. Twenty-three to be exact. I am glad I was there to pick up the pieces when Sarah found out their precious news.

"Age is nothing to do with it," I said.

"You say that, but you'll notice it from now on. Everywhere you go, there'll be a bunch of twenty-year-old girls having more fun than you. They go around in groups, hunting. They're the danger. You're ok, you have a man who adores and would do anything for you. I've got a battle on my hands now."

"Well, Alessandro didn't seem to notice any of the twenty-year olds stood around us in their miniskirts. He only had eyes for you. Text him if you want. We can meet him tomorrow evening. I don't mind."

"Are you sure? I don't want you feeling like a gooseberry."

"I'll be fine. Just tell him to meet us somewhere near the hotel so I can go back if I want to. I can always give Zack a call." And try out phone sex.

"Ok, but I'll text him in the morning. I don't want to seem too eager."

The sun was setting. It was still humid outside but this place had air conditioning so we were nice and cool inside. Sarah picked up the last slice of pizza so we could finish our feast. It was not long until I was full and bloated. The anti pasti, the salads, the bread and finally the pizza. I could not eat another bite. Zack might not recognise me when I get back as I will have gained a hundred pounds with all this bread, pizza dough and cheese. I'm sure he wouldn't mind helping me to burn it off though.

"Your meal is good, si?" Our waiter, Matteo, returned. He was the only English speaking waiter at the restaurant. He was funny although it was sometimes difficult to understand him. Or to get him to understand us.

"Si, yes, it was perfect, thank you."

"You like tiramisu?"

"Oh no, thank you," I said. "We're too full."

"You no like tiramisu?" He pretended to get upset and wiped a fake tear from his eye. "My nonna make it. You make a me sad."

"No!" I laughed. "We do like tiramisu. We're too full." We rubbed our bellies for effect. Hoping he would understand.

"You like tiramisu?"

"Yes!" We both said together.

"Ok, ok, you insist then I bring." He smiled in victory, giving me a wink.

"We will need to do a lot of walking tomorrow to burn all of this off." I said to Sarah as Matteo removed our plates.

"That won't be a problem, I'm sure!" she pulled out her phone and opened up the Rome app. "Look where we can go!"

5

"I think I'm still full from last night," Sarah said. "I can't eat any of this. I think I'll burst."

We stared at the food on our little table whilst sitting out on our little balcony. Leonardo had brought us a selection of pastries, fruit, bread and jam and Maria followed with our coffees. She seemed less angry this morning. She even managed to give us a smile which was surprising as we were still in our pyjamas.

"I know, but it looks so good. And not a biscotti in sight." I picked up one of the bread rolls and cut into it, smothering it in butter and homemade jam.

"How can you eat more bread after all that last night?" Sarah asked as she picked up a banana. "I'll have a banana, but I just don't think I can manage anything else."

"You might as well eat and fill up now whilst you can. If we're out walking in the touristy places then food will cost a fortune." I bit into the bread. This must be homemade too. It was so soft, almost like candyfloss the way it melted in my mouth. "We can eat properly tonight."

She agreed it was a good plan and decided to have a pastry. It was still early, but the sun was now up and shining down the narrow road and on to our balcony. We watched as the locals set about their days as we sat back in our chairs with our feet up on the railings. Sarah and I had been on a lot of holidays together, but so far, this was the most grown up holiday to date. We were hangover free and up early enough for breakfast.

"So, where are you making me trek to today?" I asked as we were finishing up breakfast.

"How about we walk in the direction of the Trevvi Fountain?"

"Sounds good, but how far is it?"

"Erm, just a little further on than the Pantheon, so not too far." She studied the map on her phone. "Ooh! We can do a circle and check out the Coliseum on the way back, seeing as we didn't get to see it yesterday. That will fill our day."

"Let's do it. I might have to wear my trainers today though. Those sandals I brought are great for lounging around but not walking long distance." I glanced at the blister that was threatening to burst by my big toe.

"I thought that too. You'd think we'd be used to trekking on rough terrain after all those nights out in town."

"Right, let's get dressed and go. I'll have a quick shower and you can text Alessandro."

"I can't text him now, it's far too early."

"I'm sure he's awake. Message him. Exactly what we discussed last night. 'Hello, this is Sarah from yesterday.

Thank you for the advice on where to eat. How about meeting for a drink tonight? X' Something basic and not too pushy."

She hesitated as she held her phone in her hand. Thoughts were running through her mind. The more she thought about it, I knew the less likely the message would get sent.

"It'll be fine," I said. "Don't overthink this. You're not proposing anything serious. It is just a drink. A harmless drink."

I left her with her thoughts and grabbed my phone on the way to the bathroom. There was a message waiting for me from Zack.

"Good morning baby, I hope you slept ok. Bing slept on my chest and wasn't budging this morning no matter how much I tried to move, and now I'm late for work. He must be missing you. As am I. What are your plans today? Xxx"

"Hey you," I began my reply. "I've just eaten my weight in food again so heading out for a long walk to burn it off. Tell Bing I miss him too! Xxxx"

"I hope you're missing me as well Xxx"

"Nah, far too many sexy Italians to stare at here. I might bring one home with me :P Xxxx"

"Bring one that can cook then, cremated food is not nutritious Xxx"

"That burnt lasagne was a one off! Cheeky! Anyway, I'm about to hop into the shower, speak soooooooon, love you Xxxx"

I was still wearing my giddy schoolgirl grin as I got in the shower. It was so nice to have a boyfriend who wasn't so insecure and that I could joke around with like that. My high school boyfriend, Peter, hated anyone talking to me of the opposite sex. He was so possessive. Like the time he dragged me along to a party where I didn't know anyone. It didn't stop him leaving me on my own all night. Two lads approached me and were chatting away harmlessly. After twenty minutes, Peter appeared. He didn't speak though, or pull me away. He just walked up to me, kissed me, and then left again. It would have made less of a statement had he just pissed on my leg to mark his territory. Had I known then that insecurity meant a cheating bastard then I would have left him long before I did. If only Jeremy Kyle had been around in those days to educate me.

We set off walking in our comfy trainers just after nine o'clock. Once again, Sarah's hair was elegantly flowing in the light breeze, slipping off her shoulders as she walked, and mine was already starting to stick to me. I knew wearing it down would be a bad idea, so I pulled the spare bobble off my wrist, quickly tied it all back and pulled out my fan to waft my neck.

"Has Alessandro replied yet?" I asked.

"No, not yet. He probably won't. I bet he was just being nice to the two lost tourists last night. He won't have been serious about meeting up."

"Of course he was! Why else would he give you his card? He'll reply." I still wasn't used to seeing Sarah lacking in confidence and being so down on herself. "Sarah," I held out my arm to get her to stop walking and turn to face me, it was pep talk time. She was struggling to make eye contact with me. "You've been through one of the worst years ever. First, Max The Wanker ends it. Second, you find out he's knocked the tart up. Third, he fucked up the mortgage payments so you had to move out of your dream home. You deserve to have some fun now. You deserve to have a hot Italian guy flirt with you and take you out. He *will* reply, and tonight you are going to transform back into my fabulous friend Sarah, and you will take back your happiness. It's been gone for too long, and I miss my friend Sarah. She has to make her comeback."

A small tear made its way down her cheek. She wiped it away and managed a smile before finally looking into my eyes.

"Yes, you're right. I've sulked for long enough. It's time to move on."

"Yes, it is. I'm always here if you need to talk, but you need to get back on the horse. Now, let's get to the fountain. My feet aren't aching yet so you've got plenty of time before I start moaning."

I linked my arm inside hers and we carried on with our journey with silent smiles on our faces.

"What do you mean you have to move?" I asked Sarah, as she frantically cried down the phone to me.

"Max hasn't been paying his half of the mortgage," she took a deep breath. "And he had all letters directed to his new place so I haven't known about any of this until now."

"What does your letter say?"

"That I have thirty-one days to vacate. On my thirty-first birthday I get thirty-one days to vacate. What am I going to do?"

"Don't you have any rights? You kept to your share of the payments."

"Apparently not. I called them this morning. They don't care about personal disputes. They just want paying or they repossess the house. There's no way I can pay all this."

"What an absolute cock womble!"

"I'm going to be homeless!" she cried.

"No, you're not. You can stay with me. I can clear some space in my spare room for you. Stay for as long as you need to."

"Oh, thank you." She struggled to talk through the tears. "I can't believe it. I'm losing my home. First my fiancé, and now my dream home. What else can that guy do to me?"

The Trevvi Fountain was, in a word, amazeballs. Or as the Italians would say, 'amaze-a-balls-a'. There are no other words to describe it. We stood in silence for what felt like hours and hours, just taking in all the detail.

"Well," Sarah said, "now that's a fountain."

"It sure is." Sarah's words had managed to bring me out of my trance and I had a quick look around to see who else had come here to view this masterpiece.

Above the sea of heads were iPhones on selfie sticks, like balloons on strings floating above us. No one seemed to be taking in the sight, they were just looking through the cameras on their phones. Well, the younger lot were. The older generations were enjoying it like us. Oh my god, are we now classed as the older generation? Hell no. I pulled out my phone and started snapping away, taking photos of the fountain and the odd selfie, some of Sarah and me and then Sarah on her own. Then, through the camera on my phone, I spotted it. A horrifying scene.

On the other side of the fountain, I could see a man down on one knee with a ring in hand, holding it up to a very emotional and happy woman in her twenties. Shit. Sarah doesn't need to be seeing these levels of romance. This holiday was supposed to make her forget that it was her wedding week. We have to move. She can't see this.

I turned back around to Sarah to suggest we start our walk to the Coliseum when I saw the huge, beaming smile on her face. She was looking at her phone.

"Alessandro replied," she said. "He's going to meet us later."

6

By the time we got back to our hotel, my feet were throbbing. I should have been more prepared for this trip, my feet just can't cope anymore. We must have walked at least ten miles today, in circles, going back and forth to see things we had missed. I can't complain really, Rome is spectacular. And once Sarah received that text from Alessandro, she was practically bouncing from place to place. I was struggling to keep up with her.

"We can try the bus tomorrow, if you like?" Sarah said as she watched me cringing as I took my trainers and socks off. "It might help our feet to recover."

"Definitely, ahh." A blister on my little toe had popped and the sock felt like it had been cemented to it. "Oh, that stings." The things we do for friends.

It had just turned five o'clock. We had two hours before we were meeting Alessandro at the bistro down the street. I had two hours to soak my feet in the hope that they would forgive me. I have put them through some tough times in my life, but this was almost their limit.

"Are you getting another shower?"

"I think I will." Rome in June was proving to be a hot one. Especially when you are walking around as much as we are. "Shall I go first?" I asked.

"Yes, I'll try to get online and book tickets to the Coliseum."

We had arrived at the Coliseum this afternoon, hoping to get in, but we had never seen queues like it. The worst queue I had ever witnessed until now was the day the final *Harry Potter* book was released in Waterstones, but this one was unbelievable. There was no way in hell we would have made it before it closed. And with the sun belting down on top of us, it wouldn't have taken long for us to melt. We had heard an older couple in the queue arguing with each other because the wife had apparently told the husband to book the tickets online, but the husband didn't, because he insisted she had not told him to do anything of the sort. The husband then got an earful, before loudly asking a passing tour guide if the lions were still in the pits so he could throw his wife in. They both looked miserable in each other's company.

If Zack and I ever get married and grow old together, I hope I don't turn into such a nag that he hates being around me. I want him to want me, and to be happy with me forever, and to pre-book tickets when I tell him the first time so we never end up arguing in a queue like that.

Before I stood up from the bed, taking deep breaths in anticipation of the pain that was sure to shoot through my feet as soon as I placed them on the floor, I had a quick glance to the coffee table as something caught my eye.

"Is that new biscotti?"

On a white plate with gold decorating the edges was a full plate of chocolate biscotti.

"That woman is a biscotti baking machine!" Sarah said, picking one us and taking a bite. "Wow, these ones are good."

"Anything made of chocolate is good," I hobbled to the table and helped myself to one. Sarah was right, these were delish. The last batch had barely been touched as they were rock hard and had too many almonds. Or were they nuts? I have no idea, but they weren't that great. I suspect these ones won't last the night. "Right, I won't be long in the shower. Then you can start glamming yourself up." I winked at my nervous friend and took my hot, swollen feet to the bathroom and felt sudden, instant relief as I stepped on the cold marble floor.

"I have heard of Halifax," Alessandro said to Sarah. "I visited London some years ago and saw Halifax."

"Oh, Halifax isn't in London," Sarah said.

"Hmm, are you sure? I remember a sign, with a big blue cross." He held his arms in from of him to form an 'x' shape.

"Ah I think you mean the bank. There will be a lot of Halifax Banks in London."

"Ok, ok," he seemed embarrassed, "I am sorry, my mistake. In that case, I have not seen Halifax."

"That's ok," Sarah said, "it's an easy mistake to make." They were staring into each other's eyes like two teenagers scared to admit they fancied each other.

Even though I have my own sex God at home, I can still appreciate how gorgeous this man is. He must be in his thirties. He dresses very smartly and seems quite well off. I tried to pay for a round of drinks for us but he would not allow it. I liked him even more then.

Conversation between him and Sarah was flowing nicely. He spoke really good English. I don't actually mind that I am playing the gooseberry this evening. Sarah had lost her twinkle after Max The Wanker broke her heart, her eyes had seemed dark and empty, but this evening they are shining again, and I can feel her coming back to me. Apparently, the cure to a broken heart is a sexy Italian man.

As happy as I am to witness Sarah's comeback tour, I realise it is getting quite late, and I wouldn't mind phoning Zack for a quick chat if I wouldn't be missed. Alessandro stood up.

"I will be back, mi scusi, ladies."

He wandered to the back of the bistro to the gent's toilets.

"Oh my god, Jen, how's my hair? Do I have anything in my teeth? Is my makeup ok?"

"You look like a train wreck."

She slapped my leg.

"I'm being serious! He is so yummy and I feel like a sweaty, horrible slob."

"Sarah, you look fabulous. Your hair is glossy and enviably perfect despite the humidity. Your makeup hasn't moved and he seems so besotted with you. He hasn't taken his eyes off you. Enjoy it."

"Ok, ok. I just feel so awkward chatting and flirting with a guy. I've not done this for years. I feel so out of practise. This is the first guy since, you know who, that I haven't wanted to kill."

"Well, you're doing amazing for someone who up until now has wished death on anyone with a penis. Including Santa."

"That pervert deserved what he got."

I don't think I will ever forget the image of horrified children as Sarah threw eggnog in the face of the poor Santa who was handing out candy canes and sweet words of Christmas cheer last December. *"And here is one for the pretty lady, Merry Christmas"* is all he said as he handed some candy to Sarah with a cheery smile. One eggnog shower later and were both escorted out of the Trafford Shopping Centre by security. We have not been back since.

"Well, anyway, you're doing great this evening. I was single for years and never managed to stay as calm and collected as you when I was around someone I fancied."

Alessandro appeared back at our table.

"Shall I get more coffee?" he asked.

"Oh, no thanks. I think I'll go back to the hotel actually." I looked at Sarah. "I can phone Zack and say goodnight. Is that ok?"

"Yes, sure, that's fine." She said.

"I will make sure she get back safely, do not worry." Alessandro said.

Seeing as the hotel was approximately twenty metres away from here, I was sure she would be fine.

"Ok, thank you so much for the drinks." Alessandro leaned in and did the European 'kiss on each cheek' thing. Damn blushing! "I'll see you back at the hotel." I said to Sarah, giving her a sly wink before leaving.

I walked into the hotel entrance and was met by Maria. She must have been on the wine. Her cheeks were rosy and she seemed very happy to see me, pulling me in for my second 'kiss on each cheek' of the day. She was speaking to me but I have no idea what she was saying. All I could make out whilst she held on to my hands was 'bella ragazza inglese' which I assume means 'I made you more biscotti'.

"I'm going to bed, Maria. Very sleepy."

"Ah, si si, go sleep." She smiled. "I bring more biscotti tomorrow."

"Oh, we would love more of the chocolate biscotti please. They're our favourite."

"Chocolate?"

"Yes, the ones you left for us this afternoon. There aren't many left."

Her alcohol-pink cheeks turned into furious-red cheeks. She still had hold of my hands and was tightening her grasp. I feared they would crush in her Hulk-like grip. Just at that moment, a sheepish looking Leonardo appeared.

"Biscotti al cioccolato?" she said to him, releasing her hold of my poor hands. "Bastardo!"

And then, world war three was declared right in the lobby. Maria was winning the battle for sure. I felt very awkward as Maria's argument was very animated with a hand gesture for every angry word. Italians seemed to have their own sign language for getting a point across. Maria didn't need to bother though. Anyone without sight and hearing could tell she was angry.

Maria finally stormed out of the room and into the kitchen, where more banging and cluttering followed. Leonardo looked at me unphased and smiled.

"I am sorry, Maria no like chocolate biscotti. I make them for English lady guests. They are popular. But Maria no like it. She, ah, she want to make traditional."

"I'm so sorry if I've got you into trouble!" I was mortified and scared for him.

"It no bother," he smiled. "I bring you more in the morning." He winked, and turned to go through a different door, far away from Maria. I pulled my phone out of my bag and typed a message to Sarah.

"Don't rush back. Maria is on the rampage and I got Leonardo in trouble! Whatever you do, don't bring up the chocolate biscotti!!! I'll explain later. Enjoy the rest of your evening. Have fun! ;) Xxx"

Getting back to the safety of the room was a relief. It was peaceful, away from the noise of Maria's wrath and also cool thanks to the air conditioning. I slipped off my sandals and curled up on the small couch whilst scrolling for Zack's number in my phone. I don't even know if he is free for a phone call. He could be out.

"Hey you." His voice was like music to my ears. "Everything ok?"

"Hey! Yes, it's all good here. Just thought I'd check in. Are you alright? Are you free for a chat?"

"Yeah, I've just got to yours to let Bing in and give him some food."

"How's he doing?"

"He's great, he's barely left me alone since I walked in with him. I've just been out for tea with my Mum and Dad. All they did was talk about you. They can't wait to meet you, I think they like you already."

I was looking forward to meeting them too. They live in Spain for most of the year but have come home for a couple of months to see family and friends, and I suspect escape the southern Spanish heat.

"Unlucky for you, that means you can't dump me for a young, hot blonde."

"I know. Dammit. Had my eye on one too."

"Well, my hot blonde is currently out having drinks with her new Italian boyfriend so looks like I'm stuck with you too."

"Sarah is out with a guy?" his flirty tone came to a sudden halt. "On her own?"

"Yeah. She's a grown up now so doesn't need minding."

"How long has she known him? Is it safe? You're in a foreign country you know, anything could happen." I knew it was a mistake watching *Taken* with him.

"Baby, it's fine. She will be fine. He's a nice guy and it's making her happy. Which is what this holiday is all about."

"Hmm."

"Anyway, the café they're at is literally across the road. If I lean far enough over the balcony, I'll be able to see them staring into each other's eyes feeding amaretto to each other."

"If you say so."

If this is Zack's attitude to a mature, grown up date in a foreign country, then it might be best he never hears about the girl's holiday to Zante in 2010. He would not approve.

"So, how was dinner with your parents?"

"Same old, same old. They asked about you, about work, more about you. They want me to organise a meal out with us and them if that's ok?"

"Of course it is. I can't wait to meet them. We can sort it out when I'm back."

"Good. I'll let them know. Anyway, why are we talking on the phone as if it's the nineties? Call me on video messenger, I want to see those white bits."

7

Leonardo brought us our breakfast at exactly seven-thirty the next morning. I was glad he survived the night unscathed. I couldn't help worrying about him. On the tray, along with our coffees and pastries, was another plate covered with a napkin. He placed the tray down on the coffee table and winked at me with a cheeky smile, putting his finger over his lips instructing me to keep it a secret.

When he was gone, and the door firmly shut, I pulled back the napkin and saw half a dozen chocolate biscotti. I quietly giggled and shook my head. When Sarah got back late last night, I explained biscotti-gate to her and that we would be avoiding Maria as much as possible before leaving to go home.

"Sarah, breakfast is here if you're wanting any before we head out."

"Ok," she called from the bathroom. "I'll be two ticks."

I poured us both some coffee and went straight for the biscotti. There was a hint of amaretto in the flavour this time. I need to take some of these home with me. I wonder if I could sneakily ask Leonardo for the recipe.

Sarah emerged from the bathroom, smiling to herself.

"Still smiling from last night? Must have been a good one."

"Alessandro has just texted me, wishing me a good day. That's all." She slid her phone in to her back pocket.

"Are you seeing him again? We leave in two days, you might never see him again."

"I think he wants to take me for dinner tomorrow night, he's checking his work schedule but it will be our last night here so I'm not sure. It should be us doing something special."

"We can go for dinner anytime. If you want to see him, go and see him."

"I'll see." She picked up a biscotti and dipped it in her coffee. "Oh, that reminds me," she put her drink and biscuit down and went over to her bag, pulling out some pieces of paper. "He gave me these, they're bus tickets."

"Ok," who said romance was dead?

"You need to buy bus tickets before you get on the bus or you can get fined. He buys loads in advance so he's never short of one. He just said to make sure we get them validated on the buses and we'll be fine."

"Oh great stuff. I don't fancy spending the night in an Italian police cell. Keep them safe."

She put them safely in her purse and back into her bag. She had promised me a day off from walking so those tickets will come in very handy today.

"Did you ask him which bus we need to get to the Coliseum?"

"Yes, I wrote it all down in my phone. I've got the entry tickets downloaded to my phone too. Let's eat quickly, I booked our entry time for nine-thirty and we need to be at the ticket desk thirty minutes before that, according to the app."

I picked up another biscotti.

"Eat something proper, we won't be eating once we're in there and I don't know how long we'll be in."

"Yes mum," I said, picking up another biscotti and shoving it in my bag. Oh, the life of a rebel.

Sarah, being the more sensible of us this morning, picked up the pastries and wrapped them in tissue, putting them in her bag for us. Her phone buzzed. She pulled it out of her pocket to read the message. Judging by the grin on her face, it was a good one.

"It's Alessandro, he can't do tomorrow but was wondering if I want to have dinner tonight instead." She bit her bottom lip and sat down on the bed. "What do I say?"

"You say yes!"

"Are you sure you don't mind? It is supposed to be our girly getaway. I feel awful abandoning you."

"Well, why don't you suggest that we all eat together and then I can come back here with an excuse of being tired or something."

"No, I'll tell him that you and I are eating together but we can meet for drinks afterwards."

"That sounds perfect."

She made her arrangements with her Italian man-friend and then we finished getting ready for our outing and finding a bus stop. Sarah had all the information on where we were going, so I was just following her. Her mood had definitely lifted since arriving here. Max The Wanker had done a good job at breaking her spirit. First, the affair. Second, losing her dream home. Third, the pregnancy.

I arrived home from work later than normal. I had been stuck with a customer who just wouldn't stop talking. Eventually, Sam stepped in to finish the meeting for me so I could leave. Then I hit every set of roadworks possible on the way home. Why do they all come at once?

"Sorry I'm late!" I called to Sarah. She had been staying at my house for the last three weeks since being forced to leave her home. I had been working overtime trying to keep her mood up as much as possible. We'd had an amazing Christmas, despite the Santa incident, and we threw a New Year's Eve party together. It was just like when we lived together at uni. "How about fish and chips for tea? I can nip out." I hung my coat up in the hallway and walked into the living room, but she wasn't there. "Sarah? Are you in?"

I walked into the kitchen, but she wasn't there either. She can't be too far away, Minnie was outside.

"Hello?" I called out again.

"Here." A muffled voice came from upstairs.

I immediately thought of her house offer. She had found a bungalow not far from here that she loved. It was the perfect size for her and affordable thanks to the bank of Mum and Dad. I hope it hasn't fallen through at the last minute. That is not the kind of news she needs right now.

"Where are you?" I walked up the stairs and into the spare room where she had been staying. She was sat at the end of the bed. Her tear stained face was red and blotchy. "What's happened? Is it the house?" I sat down next to her and put my arms around her, but she didn't say anything. She just stared at the wall. "Sarah, talk to me. What's happened?"

"It's not the house."

"Then what is it?" I was wracking my brain wondering if she had told me about an elderly grandparent that was ill, or if it was that time of the month.

"Max."

"What has that wanker done now?"

"She's pregnant."

"Who's pregnant?"

"The child bride he left me for. He's got her pregnant. Stupid, fertile child."

Ah. Max's twenty-three-year-old girlfriend was knocked up. Damn.

"Oh, I see."

"He told me he didn't want children. 'They tie you down' he said. Didn't want them interrupting his career, so I was the moron who had the implant all these years to keep him happy. I wanted kids. I couldn't wait to have kids. I put it on hold for him and his fucking career which he's packed in. He's not even moving to Canada anymore. They're staying here to raise their mutant baby and I am just single, thirty and childless."

"Look, you can't think about that now. Don't get worked up over what he's doing. I told you at the start of this break up that things will get worse before they start to get better."

"Losing my home was supposed to be the worst part. That should have been it. Things were supposed to be on the up now. I'm this close to getting the keys to my new house. I even got that promotion at work last week. Two steps forward and ten steps fucking backwards." She scrunched up the tissues and threw them at the bin, missing.

"Hey, you have taken a hundred steps forward over the last few months. Look at you! You're buying a house on your own, proper independent woman!"

"You've owned your own house for years."

"Not quite the same. I inherited half of it from my Dad and bought the other half from my brother. It was hardly a battle. Plus, you've just been promoted with a *huge pay rise. Yes, you want kids, but can you imagine if you'd had them with that wanker? You'd now be a single mum sharing a bed with it in my spare room. You had a massive escape from an even bigger disaster."*

She sighed.

"You shouldn't be upset that he's knocked her up, you should be sad because that poor child will be raised by him and his child-bride in her ex-council flat in that awful estate."

She managed a little laugh.

"Look at the bigger picture. Look at what is going on in your life at the moment. That should be your main focus. We need to plan on decorating your new house, shopping for furniture and knick-knacks. But most importantly..." I had a serious look on my face and waited until she looked at me, wondering what I was going to say. "Most importantly, what do you want from the chippy?"

I am pleased to report that the Italian buses felt a lot sturdier and safer than the taxi ride we had experienced from the airport. It was packed full of people and we just managed to find two seats together at the back. It was warm and sticky with all the body heat around us so I pulled out my trusty fan whilst Sarah was engrossed in her phone.

"Don't forget, you're the map," I reminded her whilst wafting myself. "I don't know where we're getting off. Keep your head up."

"That's what I'm doing." She showed me her phone. It was a map of the town and the red dot in the middle, which I could see was moving along the roads, was us. It was heading towards a blue dot. "The blue one is where we need to get off."

"Fab. Although, it's so bloody warm on here it might have been cooler if we'd walked."

"Don't say that now, we have all these tickets to use up."

It took only five more minutes to arrive at our destination. We pushed our way through the sweaty folk crowded on the bus, holding our breath from all the delightful smells of people, and finally made it out into the fresh air. We were in the shade and a welcome breeze blew under our arms, relieving us of some of the early morning heat. Maybe coming in winter would have been more sensible.

We had exited the bus on one of the older, less touristy streets of Rome, so we were glad when we found a small shop that did not charge us the earth for a bottle of water. We grabbed one each and after a difficult attempt at a chat with the Italian owner, he convinced us to buy a hat each too.

"No roof!" He managed to say, talking about the Coliseum. "The sun, on your head? Hot. Bad."

Two bottles of water, two hats and another handheld fan for Sarah later, we were ready. We thought he had just conned us into spending more money, and then we saw the

Coliseum. He was right. There was no sign of shade so we would have had the sun beating down on us for our entire visit.

We had ten minutes until we needed to be at the ticket counter, so we stood and stared at the structure. I am not a fan of history, it never interested me at all, but even I could appreciate this sight. It just took our breath away. Once again, there was a wave of cameras and selfie sticks around us. Even through it was early, there was a huge queue of people wanting to get inside.

"And that is why we booked our tickets," Sarah said. "Come on, lets head to the ticket counter. I want to see if there is a guidebook to buy."

8

"Jenny, you would love my village," Alessandro said whilst we were having our drinks together that evening. "Is a small village, everyone is family. And they all want to feed you. So, if you want to go for a walk, go at night so no one see you. Or else, you must eat *another* bowl of pasta." Sarah and I had been laughing at his stories all evening. "That is why I leave to come here. My health! You cannot say no to a Nonna with food."

"Well, tell me how to get there. That might be my next holiday."

"If you love food, move to Italy. Everyone want to feed you."

"There's my life goal," I said. "I'll need to convince Zack to move with me though. Oh crap, what time is it?"

"It's almost nine o'clock." Sarah checked her phone for me.

"Bugger. I said I'd call him at nine. I'll leave you guys to it, if that's ok?"

"We can walk you?" Alessandro stood up.

"No, no it's fine. It's only down the road." I stood up and grabbed my bag. "Thank you so much for the drinks again, it's been great meeting you."

"You too, Jenny." He kissed both of my cheeks.

"I'll see you back at the hotel," I winked at Sarah before leaving the bar. I pulled my phone out of my bag and called Zack.

"Hello." I love his voice.

"Hey you."

"Hey you too, not long now. It feels as though you've been gone for ages."

"I know, tell me about it. I can't wait to see you. Have you missed me?"

"You know I have. Being in your bed isn't the same without you there too. Bing is alright for company but his services as a cat are limited."

"Aw Bing! I've missed him too."

"Why are you out of breath?"

"I'm on my way back to the hotel." I had a slight sprint to my step. "We met Alessandro after dinner for drinks at a bar. I've left Sarah with him. He's so funny. They're really getting on. You won't believe how much she's changed since meeting him."

"She likes him then?"

"Yes, I think so. They look good together too. I think he is just what she needs to bring her out of her slump."

"I'm glad to hear it. Are you back at the hotel yet?"

"Just about, I'm just walking up the steps now. Need to try and avoid Maria if I can…"

I opened the door slowly and peeked in. There was no one about.

"There's no one here," I whispered, "I'll make a run for it to the stairs. Hang on."

I just managed to close the door when Leonardo appeared.

"Oh, hi…" I began.

"Shh," he put his finger to his mouth again and handed me a package. "Put in your suitcase." After he handed me the parcel, he quietly shuffled through the kitchen door.

"You ok?" Zack asked.

"Yeah, my new adopted Granddad appeared and has given me a small parcel."

"What's inside it?"

"I don't know for sure, but I have a sneaky suspicion." I sprinted up the stairs and made it into my room, almost dropping the phone whilst fishing about in my bag for the key. I sat down on the couch and put the parcel on the coffee table along with my phone on loudspeaker. I unwrapped the thin cloth and there was a large batch of chocolate biscotti. "Ha! Fab!"

"What is it?" Zack asked again.

"It's a load of chocolate biscotti. Bless him! Now you'll be able to try some. There's loads of it though, it might push my luggage allowance over the limit. I'll have to give Sarah half of it. Unless he has another batch for her too." Which I secretly hoped he did.

"How much have you eaten on this trip?"

"You won't recognise me. I've gained enough weight to throw the plane off balance. You won't fancy me anymore but its tough tits because you already said you love me."

"Will it seem shallow if I dump you then?"

"I'm afraid so."

"Tut, fine, but you're sharing that biscotti with me. We can be fat together."

Zack was good for a laugh, and loved to try and wind me up, but I did sometimes worry that he could stop fancying me if I gained too much weight. I know I lost weight last year after my fallout with takeaways, but it quickly piled back on when we started eating out a lot and having cosy nights in with chocolate and sweets. Relationships are great, but once you get happy and comfortable, the weight seems to creep up on you. Also, I couldn't get Sarah's words out of my mind about the twenty-year olds. They're young and gorgeous and obsessed with image with special thanks to

Instagram and *Love Island*. Plus, they're all turning vegan which means they live on grass so weigh as much as a strand of hair. Do I still need to compete with them? Look at Max The Wanker. He was in a happy relationship with my amazing friend Sarah who would have done anything for him, not to mention she is absolutely stunning, but his head was still turned by a twenty-something.

I wrapped the biscotti back up and decided to skip on more indulging this evening.

"So, what have you been up to today?" I asked.

"I called back at home today to make sure the place is still standing. It's fine. My housemate hasn't burnt the place down yet. It's been a boring one really. How was the Coliseum?"

"Oh, it was amazing. There was some serious eye porn. I took so many photos. I'll have to show you when I see you but they just don't do the place any justice at all. You won't believe how big it is."

"Well, actually…"

"What?"

"I've got a confession. I've been before. Years ago, we went as a family and did the whole touristy thing."

"Why didn't you tell me? I've been bragging about how amazing my day was and you've already experienced it. I bet I sounded like a right idiot."

"Well you can't help that," he laughed as I swore at him, "but its fine. Rome is just… there are no words for it.

Everyone needs to visit Rome at some point in their lives. And I love hearing how much you've enjoyed your break. Did you see the Vatican too?"

"Yes, we went after we had some lunch. That was a strange experience. I probably can't describe it properly, which doesn't matter as you've already been. But it felt quite eerie."

"I thought that too."

I took the phone to the balcony and sat down at the table. It seemed cooler in the air tonight. There was a refreshing breeze. I put my feet up on the other chair and relaxed talking to Zack about next week when we would both have the week off together. At least one of those days would be spent in bed. We have some making up to do.

I heard a familiar laugh and looked down over the balcony.

"I think I hear Sarah," I whispered to Zack, "yes, they're back, he's walked her home. Shh."

"Why are you shushing me? They can't hear me."

I spied on Sarah and Alessandro as they gazed into each other's eyes at the bottom of the hotel steps. I could only see the tops of their heads, but I knew they were smiling. He then raised his hand and stroked her cheek before leaning in for a kiss. Wow. I felt like I was in it. I could almost feel their body heat rising up and ruining the breeze keeping me cool. He slowly leaned back and stroked her face one last time before stepping back to walk away. He made it ten steps (yes, I counted) before he looked back to give her one final wave.

"I'll have to go, baby, she's on her way up."

"Are you going to gossip about kissing boys over biscotti?"

"Yes, in our pyjamas, right before we have a pillow fight."

"Oh, the image. Ok baby, I'll speak to you tomorrow. Love you."

"Mwah, I love you too."

I stayed on the balcony waiting for Sarah to get to the room. I watched as the knob turned on the door and in she came, rosy cheeked (finally!), eyes glistening and a smile from ear to ear.

"Ahem," I called out, "did you have a good evening?"

She didn't answer. She just nodded her head. No words were needed. Her sheepish smile said it all.

My Sarah was back.

9

Why does it always take forever for suitcases to appear on the conveyor belt at the airport? Seriously, what is the reason? We must have been standing here for twenty minutes waiting for our cases and they still haven't appeared. Our taxi will be leaving without us or will wait with the meter running and cost us an absolute fortune. I've been on a fair few holidays abroad and never, not once, has my suitcase been the first to appear.

"I wish they'd hurry up or we'll need to book another taxi," I moaned to Sarah who was oddly calm about the situation. I think she was still distracted by thoughts of her Italian friend.

"Don't worry about it, it'll be fine." She tried to reassure me, but I hate this part of holidays. Not just because it is over, but because the process of getting home takes forever. As soon as I check out of a hotel, I have checked out of holiday mode and just want to be back in my own house with the promise of my own bed at the end of it. As well as my own shower and my own coffee. Yes, I get post-holiday-grumps.

There was suddenly a loud clatter as the conveyor belt began to move.

"Finally!" I said. "Now just to wait for our suitcases to come out last."

I was incredibly surprised when mine and Sarah's cases were among the first to appear. That NEVER happens.

"There! You can stop your moaning now," she shoved me, playfully. "Come on, let's move to the front or we'll miss them and I'll need to listen to you moan as they make their way around again."

We were able to grab our bags without fail and wheeled them through the doors and out to the airport carpark. I was looking for an impatient taxi driver ready to charge us a fine for making him wait so long when suddenly… I couldn't believe it.

"Zack?!"

I dropped my suitcase and ran towards him, throwing my arms around his neck as he picked me up for a huge, much welcome and much needed, hug. He smelled delicious. I could just bite him. Reading *Twilight* must have brought out my inner vampire urges.

"What are you doing here?" He was still holding me up as I put my hands on his face to make sure it was really him and not an unsuspecting taxi driver who resembled him, a mirage due to my horniness.

"I'm your taxi," he smiled, looking at Sarah.

"I wanted to surprise you," she said. "As a thank you for everything you've done for me. Letting me live with you, putting up with me trying to sort my life out and taking me on holiday to Rome. I owe you so much."

"Aw, babe." Zack placed me back on the ground so I could hug my friend, trying not to get over emotional, which was difficult as I was tired and hungry.

"My Dad is picking me up so you guys can get off home." I spotted Sarah's Dad in his car waiting for her. He was on his phone but waved when we saw him. "Right, I'll leave you guys to it. Jenny, I'll speak to you soon."

We had a final hug and kiss goodbye and she headed in the direction of her Dad's car whilst Zack picked up my case and put his arm around me, leading me to his car.

"Happy to see me?" he asked as we got to his Ford Focus.

"Yes, you sneaky sod. I didn't think you could get the day off."

"Nah, I booked it off ages ago. I was going to surprise you at your house but Sarah called me last week to see if we could do this instead."

"Aw, that's so sweet!" I kissed him. It was a good, romantic, can't-wait-to-get-you-home kind of kiss. I pulled back. "Now, take me home and do me." Romance over. Now I mean business.

"Yes, m'lady. Get in the car." He slapped my bottom and I giddily jumped in the front seat.

10

Apparently, almost a week apart from your significant other turns you into horny teenagers again. Who knew? Absence makes the loins burn harder. We haven't left my bedroom since getting back yesterday. Well, apart from the bathroom breaks and quick hunt for a dressing gown so I wasn't answering the door to Imran, my takeaway man, stark naked. Although I don't think he would have minded. We've known each other a while.

Food was consumed in bed. My mother would be cringing if I told her. Food was not to be eaten in bed. Especially greasy food. I would have been getting a huge telling off for this. However, one thing I realised a few years ago, I am grown up! If I want to eat food in bed, I can eat food in bed. If I want to spend the day naked with my legs wrapped around my boyfriend whilst eating fried noodles, then I shall do that.

"What time is it?" I asked. It had to be mid-morning.

Zack reached for his phone.

"It's nearly three o'clock."

"What? How is it that time already?"

I felt like I should be up, being productive. I still had to unpack and do all my washing. Not to mention go to the shops for food. I had also promised Sarah a trip to Ikea for house things over the weekend. So many things to do, but my legs would not unwrap from my sexy boyfriend who was trapped between them. He didn't seem to mind, nor was he in a rush to get up either.

Suddenly, when all was peaceful and relaxed, I could hear my phone ringing.

"Bugger."

"Where is it?" Zack asked.

"I think it's in my bag, over there," I lifted my arm and pointed without looking. "They'll leave a message."

"Ok, but I need to get up. Do you want a drink?"

"Please, a coffee will be good but I'll come down for it."

I watched as my naked boyfriend got out of bed and put on his clothes. I seem to have gotten over my fear of the exposed penis in daylight. No longer did I mind seeing it walking around my bedroom in all its morning glory.

"I'll see you downstairs then." He smiled as he pulled up his pants and made his way out the door.

As the door opened, in came Bing.

"Hey little man," I said, holding my hand out to him. He ran over and rubbed his face in my palm, purring. "Aw, I missed you too."

I heard my phone bleep with the sound of a voicemail. It must be Sarah. I grudgingly threw back the duvet cover and got out, finding my dressing gown which was crumpled on the floor. Searching through my bag, I found my phone and listened to the message.

"Jennifer, it's your mother, why aren't you answering? I assume you're back in the country by now. Call me back."

There's nothing like hearing the maternal and loving voice of one's own mother. I think about ignoring it, but she'll only call back again. And again. And again. I may as well get it over with.

"Oh, she is alive." My mother's greeting never fails to amuse.

"Buongiorno." I say in my most Yorkshire accent.

"You got my message then? I think this is a record time for you calling me back. It usually takes three calls, a voice mail and a Hogwarts owl for you to get back to me."

"Well Bing ate the last owl you sent, so, what's up?"

"Your brother is having a barbeque at his house next Saturday. Just a small family do. I hope you're coming."

"He text me about something last week, I said I'd be there."

"And Zack? Will he be coming?"

"Erm, I don't know. Is he invited?"

"Of course he's invited. Your brother hasn't met him yet and it is about time he did. Make sure he comes too."

"Ok, but, you'll be nice, right?"

"I don't know what you mean," she said in her most innocent voice.

"So you weren't hinting about a summer wedding when you last saw him?"

"Oh." She paused. "He told you about that? I was just saying, this summer is meant to be the best in over a decade. It *would* be nice for a wedding. I didn't mean you two specifically."

"Just promise me you'll be tame and I'll see if he's free to come along."

"I promise. It starts at one o'clock. Next Saturday. Their house. You'll be there?"

"We'll be there. Now I have to go, I've got things to do."

"One o'clock."

"We'll be there!"

Trying to go to sleep at night can be challenging when you slept in late and haven't done much in the way of conventional exercise through the day. It's almost midnight and I am still wide awake. Zack is asleep next to me and Bing is curled up between my feet. I picked up my phone and browsed Facebook for a while, but there was nothing interesting going on. Instagram was the same old staged photos of air brushed beauty and inedible food.

I went through my messages with Sarah. I was picking her up first thing in the morning so we could head to Ikea at Birstall, hopefully getting there before the crowds, and then finding somewhere for lunch. There are loads of restaurants in that retail park so we shouldn't struggle.

Zack had said yes to coming to my brother's gathering next week. He said he was looking forward to meeting my brother, but I am dreading the whole thing. Andrew and I have always gotten along. As sibling relationships go, we had a good one. We never really fought as kids and I always covered for him when he was majorly hungover after a night out so our parents wouldn't suspect. Of course, he returned the favour when I started going out too. In fact, by then, he took me under his wing and showed me the best places to go. He was quite the lad's lad back in the day, but Elizabeth put a halt on that when they got together. He can no longer have a midweek beer, only on a weekend once the children were in bed. He's not allowed to eat processed meats, and he had to sell his favourite leather jacket because 'leather is cruel'. I was certain she was going to give it a proper funeral and cremation if he didn't sell it in time. He was gutted. To make up for it, that Christmas she bought him a faux leather jacket. My mother slapped me on the leg when I pointed out that it was made from plastic and so was more harmful to the planet than the genuine leather one.

I'd be lying if I said I didn't like Elizabeth. We actually get on really well, but every time she finds a new phase, I have to laugh at my brother's face as he tries to explain what they're doing and why, almost as if he is trying to convince himself as well as us.

So, next Saturday will be very interesting. I wonder what new 'save the planet' fad they will be in to now. Not forgetting their kids will be there too. Sam and Ethan are like chalk and cheese. Sam loves me as I can make him laugh with little effort, but Ethan has some sass for a three-year-old. He took a disliking to me from day nought and I'm sure he's plotting something against me. Not forgetting they have baby Cora too. Although, I don't do well with babies. You never know what they're thinking or when they're about to spew milk all over you.

11

I do believe that Ikea was put on this earth to test us. Not only is it a maze in which you have to follow the winding floor without cheating and sneaking through the gaps, but it is also a battle to navigate your way around the trolleys and prams fighting their way past you, almost knocking you into the basket full of yellow Ikea bags in the process. If you make it out of an Ikea store without needing anger management then you win a hotdog as a treat.

Sarah was happy with her purchases. After spending the last couple of weeks sleeping on a brand-new memory foam mattress on her bedroom floor, she had finally found the perfect bed for it. It would be delivered next week along with her new Pax wardrobe and drawers.

Sarah decided not to rush with any decorating or furnishing. It had to be just right. This was her new house, all hers, and so it had to be perfect. Zack came in useful with the decorating, and I am more than sure he will come in handy fitting all the flatpack furniture together too.

We decided on a Nandos for lunch. Sarah still had her gorgeous tan whereas mine must have stayed in Rome.

"Have you heard from Alessandro?" I asked.

"No," she smiled. "It was just a holiday fling, I think. It'd never work. Long distance is tough when it's another town, never mind another country. But it was such a good idea meeting up with him. Even though it couldn't go anywhere, I feel like I've been lifted out of my man-coma."

"Woo, progress!" I lifted my glass of water to toast this victory. "Here's to getting back out there."

We toasted my friend's launch back into the single life and I suddenly had the best idea.

"I know what you should do."

"What?" she asked, whilst digging into her food.

"I know what you absolutely *have* to do!"

This would be the best idea I have ever had. The timing is perfect. Plus, it would be nice to be on the other end of this exchange. There is no evil intent in my plan. Well, maybe a little.

"Are you going to tell me or what?"

I smiled, this is going to be fun.

"You have to sign up to Find Me A Date."

"Absolutely out of the question." She shoved a forkful of chicken in her mouth.

"Why? You have to! You made me do it."

"That was different, you needed a date to the wedding. I don't need a date."

"Yes you do, you need some dates to get you back in the swing of things. Some harmless interaction with some loser guys just for practise for when you meet someone you actually like."

"Why can't I just wait until I like someone?"

"Because you'll be too afraid to make a move, like I was. You're doing this." I reached for her phone before she could stop me. "You made me do it, against my will, not to mention those lovely guys you set me up with. This is payback."

I downloaded the app to her phone and opened up the profile before handing the phone back to her.

"You're not going to let it go, are you?"

"Not until you've had at least one terrible date that I can laugh at. Well, maybe two."

"Fine," she huffed and took her phone, typing in the answers to the basic questions and uploading a photo. She chose one from Rome where she is standing on our hotel steps. "There." She handed her phone back to me after a few minutes. "Are you happy?"

I studied her profile, making sure I approved of the answers when…

Ping.

"Woah, already? Check you out," I said as the app suddenly pinged with a notification of someone liking her profile.

Ping.

Ping.

Ping.

Ping.

"Let me see." She wanted her phone back, but I got the first look. I couldn't believe what I was seeing.

"Ha, typical. When I uploaded my profile, I got all the weirdos sending me crude messages, you're getting all the hot ones. Look at this one," I turned the phone for her to see, "Matthew, aged thirty-two from Leeds, Veterinary Surgeon. Unbelievable."

"Oh he looks nice," she took the phone from me. "And look at this one too! Anthony, twenty-nine from Huddersfield, Audio Engineer. Looks like he works at the local radio station. This might not be such a bad idea after all."

"Is everything ok with your food?" the waitress asked.

"Yes," Sarah smiled as I sulkily started munching on a chicken wing. "It's great, thank you."

It doesn't look like I'll be able to laugh at my friend's bad dates after all.

"Stop your sulking," she said. "We still need that codeword just in case. What shall we use?"

"There's only one word it could be." I said.

"Tea," we said at the same time as several more pings made their way through to Sarah's phone.

"Mute that thing will you, it's putting me off my lunch."

12

Zack offered to drive today but giving directions to my brother's house is far too complicated. Even Google Maps struggles to locate the postcode. Who buys a house in the middle of nowhere, miles away from the nearest tarmacked road? I think his driveway was last tended by the Romans.

They bought this house just after they got married, thanks to a hefty donation from Elizabeth's parents. The wedding, also funded by the in-laws, was held on an island off the coast of mainland Greece. Everything was magical and perfect as long as I didn't gag at all the romance. As long as the drinks were flowing for the dateless, single sister of the groom who was forced to walk down the aisle with one of the geeky groomsmen, then she couldn't really complain. The waiter, Christos, was barely old enough to serve alcohol but was quickly trained in replacing an empty glass of ouzo with a new one.

As my car rolled over their newly gravelled, private driveway, which was as long as my own street, we arrived at the house. I parked my car as far away as possible, delaying entering their perfect house, seeing their perfect children and having every family member commenting on how perfect everything was. Yes, Andrew's house is immaculate, but I remember his bedroom back home being so disgusting there was actually a mouse that lived under his wash basket. We called him Dumbledore, as he had the ability to appear and then disappear without a trace.

"It's not too late you know," I said to Zack as he unbuckled his seatbelt to get out. "We can leave now and say we couldn't make it."

"I think it's a little too late for that."

"Why?"

"Your mother has spotted us and is waving."

"Just don't make eye contact," I let my hair fall over my face to block her from view. "Come on, let's go."

"Come on," he laughed. "It can't be that bad. It's only family. If someone starts asking you those awful questions just shove some food in your mouth so you can't answer."

That was a good point. This is a barbeque. Better yet, this is a barbeque hosted by my brother and his wife. Their 'no processed meats' rule meant there would be proper beef burgers, pork sausages and strips of chicken coated in delicious flavours. I'm glad I skipped breakfast for this as there will be a mountain of food on offer. I was so worried about the people side of this gathering, I almost forgot about the food.

We got out of the car and Zack stared at the house. To be honest, it is more like a mansion. With five bedrooms, four with ensuites, two living rooms, kitchen diner with an added extension for office space and a playroom and more recently a conservatory, it was quite a sight to see.

"This is quite a place," he said, taking it all in.

"Isn't it just. Don't ask Liz about it though, she'll take you on a tour to show it all off."

The gravel crunched under our feet as we approached my mother in the doorway. She changed from a scowl to a smile as she greeted Zack with a hug and a kiss on each cheek. She reserved this kind of affection for Zack every time she saw him.

"So nice to see you again, Zack." She turned to me. "You're late."

She stepped back so we could make our way into the house. Their entrance hall was the same size as my living room.

"Nice to see you too, mother," I glanced at Zack who was still recovering from being smothered with kisses.

My tummy rumbled as the smell of food drifted through the house.

"The food is almost ready, so you're just in time."

"Oh good, I'm starving. Seriously, Zack, my brother gets the best burgers. You'll love them."

"Actually, erm, there's something I forgot to mention," my mother said, shutting the door behind us and blocking any potential exit. "Something about the food."

"What? Don't tell me they didn't get any burgers?" I complained, already wishing I was out the door.

"Not quite." She wouldn't look me in the eye.

"Mum, what is going on?"

"They're, ah…your brother and Elizabeth now eat a more plant-based diet."

"What the chuff is a plant-based diet?" Were they eating home grown daffodils and munching on the rose bush?

"They're vegan," she finally admitted.

An unplanned explosion of laughter left my mouth, only ending when I saw that my mother was being serious.

"Say what now?"

My brother. The one who lived on meat feast pizzas throughout university. The one who ordered double meat subs from Subway. The one who wanted a spit roast pig at his twenty-first birthday. No, this is a wind up. My brother is about to jump out of their coat cupboard and shout 'Gotcha!' whilst filming my mortified face.

"They've decided on a change to be healthier and more eco-friendly, so this whole barbeque has a selection of vegan food... and nothing else."

"So, they're going to save the planet by forcing everyone to eat lettuce and hummus?"

"Don't be ridiculous, it won't kill you to try it."

"Why didn't you tell me?"

"Because I know you, and you wouldn't have come at all."

She's right, of course. I wouldn't. Not after the great argument of 2012 with a hippy protesting in the middle of town over the treatment of farm animals;

"Animals should be free!' this long haired, bearded man was preaching in the middle of Halifax city centre. *"Not caged or shut away in a barn."*

"I don't fancy walking around the street and coming face to face with an angry bull, thank you, so they can damned well stay in their barns!" I shouted back at him.

That was the start of a highly animated debate. Quite a crowd gathered, and I'm pleased to say that most of the cheers were in my favour until the police moved us on.

"It's not going to be full of hippies is it?" I asked my mother, envisaging walking out to the garden and coming face to face with the long-haired preacher.

"Don't be stupid, it's just family and a few of Liz's friends. Now come on, everyone is waiting."

"I tell you now," I whispered to Zack as my mother walked ahead through the kitchen door. "If I find a stray caterpillar in my lettuce leaves, it's having a public execution as a protest."

"Wow, you do get cranky where food is concerned."

"My brother isn't vegan, I'll never believe it."

"Well there's only one way to find out. Come on. If you get through this without making a scene involving a caterpillar, I'll treat you to a big bucket of Colonel Sander's finest."

"You're on, but I can't make any promises."

We followed my mum through the kitchen, through the conservatory and out into the garden. I looked to the table where the food had been laid out. There was the obligatory salad bowl which I usually avoided but today it would by my only sustenance. Apart from a plate of corn on the cob, I couldn't make out what everything else was.

Suddenly, a little person appeared in front of me.

"Aunty Jen! Aunty Jen!" It called out.

"Hello Sam!" I picked my nephew up. "Oh, you've grown."

Sam giggled as I tickled him whilst he was trapped in my arms. His brother, Ethan, stared up at me with his possessed eyes. He definitely doesn't like me very much, but Sam was the complete opposite. He was such a rebel. Something that I am sure Elizabeth blames me for. I can see myself becoming his dealer, bringing him pork sausage rolls and chicken wings hidden in my bag.

"Who's that?" Sam asked, looking at Zack.

"That's my friend, Zack."

"Is he your boyfriend?" he asked, with a look of disgust on his face.

"He is, are you going to say hello to him?"

My crazy nephew suddenly went all shy. Zack tried to say hello, but he was having none of it, wriggling out of my grasp and running to his parents. Andrew, the new patron saint of animal welfare, turned and waved before making his way over.

"Jenny!" he greeted me with a hug. "Good to see you, sis. And this must be Zack?"

"It's nice to meet you, thank you for the invite." Zack shook his outstretched hand.

"Not a problem, pal. It's good to meet you finally," he took a swig of his beer.

"Erm, what's this?" I pointed at the bottle.

"What?"

"This, right here, you might have missed it, it says 'non-alcoholic'. I thought you were allowed to drink on weekends. Did you buy the wrong one?"

"Well, no, Elizabeth doesn't want alcohol in the house whilst she's breastfeeding. If she isn't allowed to have it then it's not really fair."

"And this whole vegan thing is, what, because the baby can't chew on a steak yet so it's not fair?"

"Actually, a plant-based diet is incredibly healthy," he spoke loudly, turning to check where his wife was. "No saturated fats, high fibre and, erm, yeah its proven to improve health. What are you staring at?"

"Nothing, nothing," I said, although I had been staring at his mouth, waiting for the lip to quiver to give him away. "So, who's here then?" I looked around, seeing a small crowd of people swarming Elizabeth as she cuddled baby Cora.

"Not many actually. Had a few people cancel last minute."

"Hmm, that is weird." Betting anything that it was the food on offer that turned off many of his pals. "Well, you'd best tell me what food there is because I have no clue what you've put out."

"Me neither," he said a little quieter, using his bottle to cover his mouth. "It's all a load of crap. I'll tell you where the sausage rolls are hidden later."

13

"See? That wasn't so bad was it?" Zack asked as he drove us home. I was too full to concentrate on driving to took him up on his offer.

"It was alright," I conceded. "Those vegan hotdogs were nicer than I thought they would be. How did you get on? I saw you chatting to my brother for ages."

"Yeah, I noticed you'd been roped into a game of hide and seek with Sam. He's adorable."

"It was fun, but I admit, I was trying to stay away from my mother. She kept trying to make me hold the baby. I mean, yes, Cora is cute, but I prefer them when they can talk." Zack laughed at me. "Do you know what I mean though? Babies are silent and you never know what they're thinking."

"You might feel different when it's your own."

His words knocked me back a bit. My own? Did he mean that I would have babies without him? Or is he planning that kind of future with me? We've never talked about having kids. We've never even talked about getting married. He has practically moved in with me since I got back from Rome. We haven't spent a night apart. I know his tenancy is up on his house share soon. Does he want to renew it or make it official and move in with me? Apparently, grown men are as silent as babies when it comes to what they're thinking.

"Perhaps," I didn't know how else to respond.

"I was chatting to your brother about holidays actually. He said they'd not been abroad since having Sam."

"No, I think the thought of controlling that many children on a flight will give Elizabeth a panic attack. Shame really. They had some fantastic holidays before they got married."

"I was thinking, why don't we go somewhere?"

"Really?" I suddenly imagined us buying a tent, camping in a boggy field and trying to heat up Heinz tomato soup over a poorly lit campfire. "Yeah, that could be nice."

"There'll be some late summer deals. Portugal is nice, have you ever been?"

"No," my mood suddenly perked up and I forgot all about my indigestion. "Have you?"

"A few times. Or we could look at the Canary Islands. Where would you like to go?"

"Anywhere that I can relax by a pool or dip my toes in the warm sea, and feel my skin sizzling under the sun," I smiled.

It may not be one of the more serious relationship questions but asking to go on holiday is a huge step forward.

This would be a very good idea. I know I've seen Zack naked, but seeing him in his swim shorts running along the beach in a Baywatch fashion was getting me excited.

"Great. We can get looking later, get some ideas." He took his left hand off the steering wheel and put it on my leg, leaving it there whilst we cruised down the motorway.

I felt my phone buzz in my pocket. I checked my new apple watch as getting to my phone would mean moving Zack's hand off my leg. It was a message from Sarah, and the message contained just one, all too familiar word. Without instruction, I knew what to do when my single friend currently on her very own blind date sent me a message saying 'Tea'.

"I forgot that Sarah was meeting someone today. She mustn't be enjoying herself much," I tried, but I couldn't contain my giggles.

"Aren't you going to call her then?"

"I'll wait until we get back to mine. It's only twenty minutes away. She needs the full experience for her first one." I settled back in my seat, imagining spending my days under the hot sun, rubbing sun cream into Zack's naked torso.

14

"What took you so long?" Sarah asked me when I called her back later that evening for the full story.

"It wasn't that long," I said. I didn't tell her there was an unexpected delay because Bing had managed to open the kitchen cupboard and polish off an entire bag of Dreamies. Zack helped me to clean up the vomit whilst Bing was evicted to the garden until further notice.

"Twenty minutes is far too long," she argued. "Oh Jenny, it was bloody awful. Just awful. So humiliating. I forgot how terrible the dating scene could be."

"Given how much I complained about it, that does surprise me."

"I couldn't get away quick enough. I am mortified."

"So, go on then, tell me what happened?"

*

Sarah walked into the Slug and Lettuce in Leeds that Saturday afternoon. She had opted to wear her floral maxi dress and her hair down, bouncing off her bronze shoulders as she strutted in her stilettos. There was a group of men in their early twenties by the bar, making the most of the two-for-one drinks offer. They all looked up as she walked in, smiling at her as she removed her sunglasses. She wondered if one of them might be Nigel, her suitor, but none of them advanced towards her. She decided to wait for him at the bar, when a tap on her shoulder stopped her.

"Oh, I don't need a table just yet," she told the young waiter. "I'm waiting for someone, so I'll hang by the bar until he gets here."

"Sarah?" the young, short man said to her. "It's me, Nigel." His braces sparkled under the chandelier light and his black bow tie looked slightly wonky against his white, creased shirt.

Sarah thought this must be a wind up. Her friend Jenny has arranged this as payback. It had to be. Nigel's profile photo depicted a normal enough looking guy in a suit, seated at a computer desk holding a tumbler glass with what looked like a shot of whiskey. She now suspected that the whiskey was in fact apple juice as he did not look old enough to drink.

"Oh, hello," she didn't know what to say as she looked down at him, noticing his shirt was not even tucked in.

"Our table is over there, by the window," he panted excitedly. Sarah looked to the group of guys by the bar, hoping they would notice a damsel in distress and save her, but they had now been joined by a group of twenty-something girls in skimpy outfits and were no longer interested in her.

Sarah followed her date, suddenly feeling like a child minder. He gallantly pulled out her chair for her which she quietly thanked him for, secretly wishing it wasn't a table by the big window but rather at the back where no one could see her.

"So," Sarah began, "Nigel, I have to be honest, you're not what I was expecting."

"Aw thanks!" he blushed, clearly taking it as a compliment. "I just had my braces changed." He smiled, showing off his sparkly, silver frames.

"How old are you?" She asked. She knew she sounded blunt, but she wasn't happy.

"I'm twenty-two. I know my profile says thirty-two, I need to change it."

"Yes, you do."

A waitress appeared with a plate of sandwiches, nibbles and cakes. Sarah was confused as they hadn't even ordered anything yet.

"I hope you don't mind," Nigel said, seeing her confusion. "I thought it would be nice to share an afternoon tea."

Sarah thought the food looked very nice. She wondered if concentrating on the food would make this date more tolerable until she was rescued.

"Welcome back Nigel! There are two glasses of prosecco included per person, as you know," the waitress began, "but as it is a special occasion," she winked at Sarah, "I'll just bring you a bottle instead."

The waitress almost danced as she walked away.

"Special occasion?" Sarah asked, wondering why he was so well known here.

"Yes, when I booked here, I said it was our first romantic meeting," he snorted, "and I wanted it to be special.

Sarah looked over at the bar and saw the waitress standing with four other staff members who were all watching this 'romantic meeting' and laughing together. Two were wiping tears from their cheeks. She knew they were laughing at her expense.

The waitress had managed to compose herself long enough to bring over the bottle of prosecco and two glasses, however the tears of laughter were still in her eyes.

"Here you are," she said, gleefully. "Is there anything else we can get you to make your time with us more memorable?"

"No," Sarah said quickly through gritted teeth. "This is memorable enough, thank you."

As the smarmy waitress walked away, Sarah poured herself a glass of prosecco and wondered what was taking Jenny so long to call her back. She had rescued her friend many times from disaster dates. It was time to return the favour.

"So, I don't know if you recognised my name, but I'm a bit of a celebrity around here," Nigel said, waiting for Sarah to ask him to elaborate. She stayed quiet, so he continued. "I write a very popular blog."

Sarah suspected that this conversation was going to be all about fan fiction for Star Wars or even comic book heroes. Maybe even Anime comics. All things that she had very little interest in and no desire to learn about.

"Oh yeah? I can't say I recognise your name," she picked up her glass. "What do you write about then?" May as well entertain him and pretend to be interested, it could pass the time, she thought as she glanced down at her Michael Kors watch, wondering what was taking her friend so long to call her. She sipped her prosecco, allowing the bubbles to tickle her nose, deciding that would be the only foreplay she would allow on this date.

"It's a sex blog."

Sarah almost choked on her prosecco bubbles as she tried to hold in a laugh. Her ears were playing a trick on her as she thought she heard him say 'sex blog'? She wondered if he meant fantasy sex as there was no way Nigel was a ladies' man. More like his World of Warcraft characters got busy in between fantasy wars.

"Sorry, I must have misheard you." She wiped prosecco from her chin with a napkin. "What did you say?"

"I write a sex blog. I write about all my personal experiences. It has a *huge* following," his hand gesture as he uttered the word 'huge' made Sarah want to laugh even more, if not vomit her prosecco back into her glass. "So, just a heads up, I am up for anything." He smiled, licking his lips.

Sarah cringed. She wanted to be sick. She wanted to leave. She wanted her best friend to hurry the hell up and call her back!

"You might be interested to know about one in particular," he placed his small hands on the table, leaning closer towards her as she instinctively leaned back in her chair. "All about small public spaces, and making the most of it," he winked at her as she tried not to laugh.

Nigel picked up one of the tuna sandwiches and took a bite, not realising some of the tuna had stuck to his chin.

"My latest blog," Sarah spotted the huge chunk of tuna caught in his braces as he began to speak with a mouthful of food, "was with my last date from Find Me A Date."

"Oh yeah?" Sarah had been put off her food and just carried on drinking, soon needing to top her glass for another.

"There are some pretty freaky ladies on there. Up for some quirky stuff. Do you want to read it?" He reached for his phone.

"No! God no. I mean, no. Not whilst we're eating."

Sarah made the mistake of looking around again. The group of guys she had seen at the bar had found a table and they were all facing her, holding up their phones to video her disaster date. She held her hand to her face, but she knew it was too late. Just like she knew she would never live down this moment. She could never step foot in this bar again, that's for sure. Which was a shame, she thought, as she loved their cocktails. She could hear whispers around her. "What are they saying?"

"Oh, they're my fans. Hey guys." He waved to them.

"Go on, Nigel!" one shouted.

"Nigel! Nigel! Nigel!" a few of them chanted.

"Got yourself another stunner there, Nigel!"

Nigel blushed as he lapped up the attention.

"They love my blog. They share it all over their social media. Great guys," he blushed.

Great, Sarah thought, as she realised she would be trending on Twitter before the night was out.

"Can I get you anything else?" the smarmy waitress returned. "Would you like to pre-order one of our desserts to share?" The waitress could see the torture in Sarah's face, but it did nothing to help her giggles.

"That sounds lovely, doesn't it?" Nigel's greasy tuna fingers reached out across the table and stroked Sarah's unsuspecting hand.

She pulled back in disgust.

"Is everything alright, darling?" Nigel looked concerned.

"No, just no. This isn't funny anymore." Her chair scraped back on the floor tiles as she tried and succeeded to make her exit from her date.

"Awwww!" echoed through the room as her expanded audience showed their sympathy for Nigel who was now standing, confused and upset. He was overshadowed by the waitress who was trying to hide her laughter from the disappointed young man.

Sarah didn't care. She was humiliated. This is not what she signed up for.

*

I was laughing so much I could hardly breathe, occasionally snorting down the phone which made me laugh even more.

"I'm deleting that app."

"No, you're not," I insisted. "It was the first date. You've popped your blind date cherry. It is time to find your second date."

"Do I have to?"

"Absolutely. This is fun, I can see why you sent me on so many. We just need a better vetting system. I'll help you find your next one. But most importantly, what is Nigel's blog link? I *have* to see it."

"I have no idea, I daren't ask. Tell me something to get my mind off the thought of Nigel touching my hand with his grubby, greasy fingers. What did you do today?"

"I ate vegan food at a vegan barbeque."

"Shut up. You? I don't believe you."

"Well, believe it. I'm even thinking of converting."

"Now I know you're lying. You'd never give up steak."

I told Sarah how my brother is now a closet meat eater who literally has meat products hidden in a cupboard in his garage for him to sneak out and eat when he'd had enough of tofu and soya. I know he's only doing it to please Elizabeth. She has a new trend to try every year. Next, she will want to live in a mud hut in the middle of the woods without electricity or running water.

"But my most exciting piece of news," I hesitated, leaving Sarah in suspense. "Zack has asked me to go on holiday with him."

"Oo! How exciting! Where will you go?" she asked.

"I'm not sure. Somewhere hot and sunny, walking distance to the beach, food on demand, balcony, private pool."

"You're not asking for much then," she laughed. "You'll get some good deals this time of year."

"Hopefully. I think we'll get looking properly over the next few weeks. We just need to get this meal out of the way with his parents."

"You're meeting the parents too? This is a night of big news. When is this?"

"I don't know, he's downstairs on the phone to them now. I'm so nervous. I get the impression they're really well off so I hope they don't suggest somewhere posh to eat. Those places always serve tiny portions of pretentious food. Do you remember your aunty Beverley's wedding in York?"

"Oh yes," she laughed, "when you made me sneak out with you to the KFC down the road before the evening guests arrived?"

"I was starving! That piece of pork was so small it would have been better served on a side dish."

"Well, find out where his parents want to take you first and check out the menu. Then eat before you go if you have to."

"That's a good idea. Anyway, we need to meet up soon and find your next date."

"Believe it or not, I'm not in any rush for that."

I joined Zack in the living room, snuggling up to him on the couch. Bing was back on his windowsill perch, hanging his head in shame.

"How'd you fancy going to Ricci's next weekend to meet my parents?"

"Oh, I love that idea," meeting them on my own turf would make me more comfortable.

"I thought you would. Mum's so excited to meet you," he put his arm around me and kissed my cheek. "So, go on, how bad was Sarah's date?"

"Hilariously bad. Wait until you hear this."

15

I am a sensible, mature, thirty-one-year-old woman. I work in customer services, actually dealing with members of the public on a face to face basis, giving them joyous news of why they can't have what they want, just because they think they're entitled to it. I have faced many obstacles in my life, not to mention living on my own all these years with a cat I was sure wanted to kill me during the first few years of being roomies. So, after all that, why am I suddenly terrified of meeting my boyfriend's parents? They're humans. Two humans who produced the love of my life. Two humans who supposedly already like me before they've even met me. Why am I so nervous?

I would be even more nervous had my favourite restaurant not been chosen for this momentous occasion. I had not been to Ricci's Place for some time. After turning over to the dark side and admitting I had enjoyed vegan food, I needed to make up to my stomach with a big, juicy steak. Although, steaks are very filling. I don't want to be burping in front of Zack's parents. What would they think of me? With names like Alistair and Miranda, they're sure to be posh. They wouldn't be happy that their only son has taken up with a commoner from Halifax with strips of steak stuck in her teeth. I may need a safer food choice this evening.

We managed to find a parking space close to the restaurant. When I got out of the car, I checked over my dress to make sure I wasn't covered in Bing's white hair. Using my phone's front camera, I checked over my make up too, not wanting my eyeliner to appear smudged. I also needed to keep my phone close by. Sarah was on another blind date, and I had promised to call her straight away if she needed to escape.

"Are you alright?" Zack asked, putting his arm around me to lead my resistant body to the restaurant.

"Yes, yes I'm fine," I lied, almost choking as my mouth and throat felt really dry.

"That's their car," Zack pointed to a silver Porsche Carrera. "Dad loves that car. Mum wanted him to sell it as it sits in a garage for six months out of the year. But he can't part with it."

"Why can't you have it?" I said, trying to stop myself from drooling all over the bonnet.

"Ha, I asked that a few years ago… Dad still laughs about it now. Come on, they'll be waiting."

He held my hand and squeezed it reassuringly and we walked up the stone stairs and through the glass door.

"Hello and welcome to Ricci's Place," the hostess greeted us. "Do you have a reservation?"

"Yes, we're meeting my parents." Zack pointed to the table near the bar where two tanned people waved at us, and the waitress led us to them.

"I'll be back shortly to take your drinks order," she smiled.

Zack hugged his parents. It was very loving and affectionate. Not something I was used to myself.

"Mum, Dad, this is Jenny," he kept his arm around his mum. I couldn't imagine doing that with my own.

"Hi, it's so nice to meet you," I almost curtsied. This was not the time to be a tit.

"Hello!" his mother stepped forward. "I'm Miranda." She pulled me in for a hug. It felt wonderful, very mumsy. "We're so glad to finally meet you!" Her smile was so genuine, and I felt instantly at ease.

"I'm Alistair," his Dad stepped forward, "would a hug seem too awkward or…" he held out his arms and I laughed.

"No, no it sounds great!" I said, leaning in to hug this jolly man.

"Let's sit and get some drinks ordered," Alistair said. "I've never been here before, but it's very busy which is a good sign."

"Jenny is a regular here," Zack said, smiling my way. "She could recite the menu if you asked."

"That's, that's not true," I said, whacking him playfully on the arm. "It's a great place. You'll love it."

"Can I get you anything to drink?" The waitress returned.

We each gave our drinks choices. Miranda and I ordered the same glass of wine so decided to share a bottle instead, and the guys ordered an Italian beer.

"Jenny," Miranda began, "Zack tells me you own your own house. Is that true?"

"Yes, it is."

"I've been telling Zack to buy a house for years, but he never listens."

"Well, it's so difficult to get on the property ladder these days," I had to defend my man. "To be honest, I was only able to buy my house because I inherited half of it when my Dad died. I got a mortgage for the other half, buying it from my brother."

"Oh, I'm so sorry about your Father," Miranda looks mortified.

"It's fine, it was a long time ago," I said, worried I was bringing the mood down on the evening. "I grew up in that house, well, until my parents split up anyway. So, when it became empty, I asked my brother what he wanted to do. He didn't want it, I did, so I bought it." I smiled.

"Sad circumstances, but a great position to be in," Alistair piped in. "You made a very sensible decision."

"Thank you." I was almost beaming. I never got the same praise of my own mother. All she could say was *"You'd best change the hallway carpet, that's where your Dad's dog died."*

Fifty minutes and four delicious plates of food later, we were all relaxed and enjoying each other's company. I can't believe I was so nervous. Miranda and Alistair are great. They're so easy to talk to and seeing Zack with them has made me love him even more. He is so respectful and polite, especially with his Mum. If a man can respect his own mother, he will always respect you. That's what my Grandma used to say. And she was right.

The conversation had moved onto holidays. Zack mentioned that we had discussed booking a break for September. We still haven't found anywhere, there is so much choice.

I felt my phone buzz in my bag. When I checked it, it was a message from Sarah, with that one famous word. It was time to rescue her. I couldn't leave her waiting again like last time.

"I'm so sorry," I said. "I just need to make a call. Will you excuse me?"

As soon as I stood up, Zack and Alistair stood up in unison. It felt like I was an important lady at the dinner table in *Downton Abbey*. How very proper.

I smiled at the hostess as I nipped out the glass door and to the bottom of the steps.

"Hello?" Sarah answered.

"Hey, it's me, there's a huge comet flying towards earth about to land on your car. You might want to park somewhere else."

"Oh no, that's terrible!" Sarah's A Level Drama was paying off. "I'm coming right now, don't move, I'll be right there. I'm so sorry," she was talking to her date now, "I have to leave. Let's rearrange, ok? Goodbye." I heard a lot of muffled noise before she came back on the phone. "I'm back, I'm outside now. Oh my god that was creepy."

"Worse than your sex blogger?"

"Much worse."

"Was he vegan?"

"Shut up," she laughed, "it started really well. I had high hopes for this one. He was a fitness instructor. Very hot body. Very nice to look at, but…"

"But what?"

"He was fitness obsessed. When we were looking through the menu and he asked me what I fancied to eat, he'd tell me how many miles I'd need to run to burn it off. But it wasn't even a fun fact, he was actually telling me I would need to burn it off because he could never be seen with a fatty, and it would be a shame to let myself go. After all, I am in my thirties so my metabolism won't be what it used to be. Those are the words he used. Can you believe it?"

"What an absolute dick!" I said a little too loudly, aware that the restaurant doors were open so I could be overheard. That kind of language isn't very *Downton Abbey*.

"Where are you? Can I come over?"

"I'm out with Zack and his parents."

"Oh, I forgot! How's it going?"

"Really well, I'll call you tomorrow and tell you, but I love them."

"Aw that's so good! Don't order any pudding, you'll need to do a good four to five mile run if you do."

"Ha ha, I won't. Speak to you tomorrow."

"Bye!"

I ran back up the stairs and arrived back at the table.

"Is everything ok?" Miranda asked.

"Oh yes, my friend needed a quick word but she's fine." I winked at Zack.

"Zack," Miranda said, putting her hand on her son's arm. "Why don't you see what Jenny thinks to our idea?"

I looked at Zack, who seemed hesitant.

"Mum has suggested that we all go away together in September. They have a villa in Crete and were already planning to go. It has four bedrooms, two living rooms, three bathrooms, tennis court. It's a shared pool but only with one other villa. Very close to the beach. We'd only need to pay for the flights. What do you think?"

"Don't feel pressured," Alistair said. "If you kids want your own holiday, that's fine by us."

"It's very private," Miranda said, "and lots of room we wouldn't need to be under each other's feet. You can both do your own thing when you like. All I ask is we try eat together a few evenings. We had a new kitchen put in last year, but there is a barbeque too."

"If you like lobster, you'll like it even more on a barbeque," Alistair said with a smile.

This sounded amazing. How could I refuse.

"That sounds like a great idea. I'd love to."

Zack beamed; he was obviously hoping I'd say yes.

"I'm so glad!" Miranda clapped her hands. Her smile stretched from ear to ear and she grabbed hold of her husband's hand. He also seemed delighted. "This calls for a toast. Shall we have one more before we call it a night?"

16

The following weekend, Zack and I were at Sarah's house helping to put together her new Ikea furniture which had finally been delivered after being delayed. Well, Zack was doing a grand job at putting it all together and I was doing a grand job of making Sarah jealous about my upcoming two-week getaway to an all-expenses paid villa in Crete. The flights were booked and I had successfully arranged time off work.

"Two whole weeks?" she said as we were sitting on her new sofa drinking wine. We were flicking through profiles on Find Me A Date, but not having any luck. "Don't say anymore, I might actually turn green."

"Did I mention it has a tennis court?"

"Since when do you play tennis?"

"Never," I sipped my wine, "but when in Rome."

"Oh, what about this one?" she handed me the phone. "Twenty-eight years old, a postman…"

"Nope," I quickly interrupted. "Postmen get up early on a morning. You don't need that alarm clock waking you up on a Monday. Next."

"But he was so hot!" She pouted. "You're so picky."

"No, I'm experienced in this app dating business. And if anyone messages you wanting to video call, tell them no."

"Are you girls ok or do you need a rest?" Zack popped his head into the room.

"Are you implying that we're not being helpful? We're being very helpful and testing out the comfort of this new couch. A very important job."

"I see," he smirked, "don't work too hard though. I don't want you to strain yourself. Sarah, I don't suppose you have any scissors?"

"Oh yes," she got up, passing me the phone. "I'll get you some." She ran down the hall and up the stairs her bedroom. I asked if it could still be classed as a bungalow if it had more than one floor. Apparently, it can.

"How are you getting on?" I asked.

"Almost there, just the wardrobe is a bit awkward." He wiped some sweat away from his upper lip.

"Do you need any help?" I felt guilty. Sarah and I had spent the whole evening gossiping whilst he got on with putting all her stuff together. To be honest, I am hopeless when it comes to this. I would only get in the way.

"No, it's fine. Won't be long now."

"Got them!" Sarah called from upstairs.

"Coming." Zack left and made his way to meet her.

I swiped through the profiles. Most of them were the same losers from when I had the app. Left. Left. Left. Woah, what? Is that who I think it is? It can't be. It is.

Dan.

I couldn't believe what I was seeing. Dan had a profile and was looking for a date. I guess he was serious about wanting to settle down.

"You look like you've seen a ghost," Sarah said as she joined me again on the couch.

"I think I have." I passed her the phone and whispered. "It's Dan."

"Dan who? Your Dan?"

"Yes."

"Oh right, how funny." She topped up our wine glasses. "Well, if he's single, he's allowed to mingle."

"I know, I just wasn't expecting to see him."

It's been a while since I've even thought about him but thinking about him now, looking to date other people, made me feel uneasy. It's always weird seeing ex-boyfriends with other people, especially when you're usually imagining them being hit by a bus, but Dan and I were never boyfriend and girlfriend. We didn't end things with an argument or a fight. We just ended.

"What does it say in his profile?" Sarah asked.

"I don't know, I haven't read it."

Sarah clicked on his profile and read it aloud.

"My name is Dan and I am thirty-two from Halifax, West Yorkshire. I work as a senior mortgage advisor. I've had fun over the years but now looking to settle down with the right girl who is also looking for love."

My heart almost melted.

"Bless him," I said. "I didn't know he had that in him."

"You had a real impact on him it seems. 'Also looking for love', sounds like you broke his heart and he needs someone to heal it."

"Don't be daft," I said. "I didn't break his heart. We just wanted different things."

"Yes, he wanted you and you wanted the hunk building my furniture." She laughed. "Can't blame you for that but let him get on with it. If he knows what he wants, and you're his friend, let him be happy."

"That's true," we clinked glasses and I remembered the all-important question I had to ask her. "Speaking of doing huge favours for your best friends, could you do one little thing for me?"

"Go on," she looked at me suspiciously.

"Please could you watch Bing for me while I'm away? Check on him every other day and make sure he has some food? I don't want to put him in a cattery."

"Why doesn't he just come and stay with me whilst you're away? He doesn't like being on his own anymore does he?"

"No, not really." He still hadn't fully recovered from his own vacation last year and goes into a panic when he is home alone for more than twenty-four hours. Only I could get a cat that suffers from anxiety and depression. "But I'm scared he'll claw at your brand-new couch or something."

"It's only two weeks, I'll leave him in the kitchen when I'm at work. You should bring him around here, it'll be fine."

"Are you sure?"

"Absolutely. It'll be a good test. Whether or not I'm ready for my own pet."

"I wouldn't measure that kind of commitment against having Bing in your house."

"Sarah?" Zack called from the bedroom. "Where do you want the wardrobe?"

"Hang on, I'll be right there."

Sarah ran out of the room and I picked her phone back up, looking at Dan's profile. It was a good photo. His hair was neatly cut and he was wearing a black shirt. He looked very grown up. Very different from the Dan I remembered. Good for him.

17

We arrived back at my house later that night. Bing had been asleep on the windowsill and ran to the door as we came through to greet us, rubbing himself on both of our legs until Zack gave in and picked him up for a snuggle.

"Do you want some Dreamies?" he said, cradling my once human-hating cat. "Come on, let's get some Dreamies."

Bing's white tail flickered from side to side at the mention of his favourite treat. Zack was so at home here now. I've been back from Rome for a few weeks and we still haven't spent a night apart. It's become normal for him to be here. I wonder if it is time to make it official. His tenancy is almost up on the flat, there's no point in him renewing it and paying rent for a place when he is never there. Should I ask him to move in? I suddenly had butterflies in my tummy. I was nervous. It is such a big step, I'm going to ask my boyfriend to move in with me. I don't know whether to cry with nerves of being rejected or smile at the idea I am going to be living with a guy for the first time in my life. Oh my, it is so grown up of me!

I walked into the kitchen and Zack was feeding Dreamies to Bing, one at a time.

"Do you fancy a coffee?" I asked, wondering how to bring something like this up.

"Please babe," he gave Bing his last treat and brushed the crumbs off his hands. "Do you fancy watching a film in bed?" He came up behind me and put his arms around my waist.

"That sounds nice," I said, "but, I was thinking, you've been here a lot lately haven't you?"

His body stiffened. Crap. This is going wrong already.

"Are you getting sick of me?"

"No! Oh my god, no." I turned to face him. "That came out so wrong. What I'm trying to say, is… what I mean, we're always together, here." His eyes widened, as though wondering where I am going with this. Hell, I don't even know where I'm going with this. Word vomit is making a tit out of me when what I really want to say is, "do you want to move in? Properly?"

His panicked face relaxed, he released a long breath and finally smiled.

"I thought you were trying to kick me out then."

"I'm sorry," I laughed, covering my face with my hands. "I'm so bad at the serious stuff. This is so new, but I want you to move in. I know you've been here every night anyway but let's make it official." It was my turn now to put my arms around his waist. "Do you want to live here? Officially?"

"Officially, yes, I do." He finally leaned forward and kissed me. "Wow, our first holiday and moving in together. This is a very grown up year for us. We're only in our thirties."

"Yeah, practically still kids."

We kissed again. I can't believe how happy I feel right now. A year ago, I never would have believed anyone who said not only would I be kissing Zack in my kitchen, but that he would actually want to move in with me. And with only a few weeks until our holiday, things could not get any better.

18

I am officially on holiday countdown. Just seven days to go. Eek! Sam has allowed me to work half a day today, or rather she is getting sick of my holiday talk and didn't put up much of a fight when I asked to leave early, so I have decided to nip home to get changed and then head to the White Rose Shopping Centre for some last minute holiday bits. There might be some bikinis in the sale. I only have seven to take with me. A few more couldn't hurt.

It's a humid day, but the air conditioning in my car keeps me cool. Zack is going straight to his flat from work to do some more packing and organising, so won't be with me for tea. I want to be healthy so I don't put on any unwanted pounds before the big holiday, but with the choice of food on offer at White Rose… McDonalds and Subway and Nandos, oh my!

I ran through my front door and threw my keys on the stairs. Bing snook outside before I had a chance to stop him.

"Bing!" I waved my hand for him to come back inside, but he just ignored me, swaying his tail from side to side on the driveway. "Oh, fine. Stay out then."

It doesn't take me long to get out of my uniform and into my blue jeggings and black t-shirt. A jacket isn't necessary in this weather. I can hear Bing crying to come in from my open bedroom window.

"I'm coming," I call to him as he wails louder than usual. He can be such a moron. He never goes out the front door. All there is for him is a crappy driveway and kids zooming up and down the road on their bikes. The back garden is the best place for him. "I'm coming Bing."

Within minutes, I'm pulling on my converse and running down the stairs to let the cat back in now he's changed his mind about being outside, but something about his cry concerns me.

"Here you are, you silly sod," I say to Bing has he runs into the hallway. He lets out a meow that sounds more like a moan. And another, louder. "What's the matter?" I drop my bag on the floor. There looks to be something in his mouth. "Come here," I kneel on the floor beside him, but he turns away from me. "Come here," I say again, getting worried. His mouth is wide open, drool is dripping on the floor. He seems agitated. Has he been bitten by something? He likes chasing spiders.

I can hear a dull buzz sound, then I see it before I can figure out what I just heard.

On the floor drops a wasp. A half dead wasp. It's pathetic attempt at flapping its wings results in my picking up my discarded boot and whacking it flat in a panic.

I look at Bing whose eyes are wide. There is a pool of drool by his feet now and he is panting heavily like he is struggling to breathe. Oh f... fiddle sticks.

Pulling out my phone, I quickly call the vets and explain what's just happened to the receptionist. She puts me on hold to speak to the vet, returning within a minute telling me to bring him in straight away. She doesn't even take my details, just tells me to get there immediately in case my cat is having an allergic reaction.

I leave Bing in the hallway so I can retrieve the cat carrier from under the stairs. He must be in shock as he doesn't move. He is hunched over now, focusing on breathing.

"It's ok Bing, it's ok." I open up the carrier, getting angry at the zips for not cooperating with my shaking fingers.

As soon as it is up, I scoop him up and place him gently inside, hearing him growl at being moved. That was an angry growl. I hope it isn't Dr Stevens on today. Please, don't be Dr Stevens.

Dr Stevens opened up the door to his treatment room and scans the waiting area full of people and their pets. He sees me and Bing but purposely doesn't make eye contact with us. He speaks to the receptionist who points our way. When he sees who has been booked for an emergency visit with him, the colour drains from his face, and he is as white as Bing's fur.

"Do you want to come this way?" he says with very little enthusiasm.

I follow him into the room, placing Bing on the table.

"So, do you want to tell me what's happened?"

I relay the story to him, describing how I saw the wasp and suspect he has been stung.

"Do you think he's having an allergic reaction?" I say, panicked.

"I'll, erm, I'll have to examine him." I can sense his apprehension. Vets are supposed to love and respect all animals, however, this is no normal animal. This is Bing. And Dr Stevens bears the scars of coming in to contact with this creature. "Has he vomited at all? Diarrhoea?"

"No," at least I couldn't smell anything going on in his carrier. "Nothing like that."

"Do you, erm," he exhaled loudly, "do you want to get him out and I can have a look. It was in his mouth, you say?" he stroked his own hand, remembering the horrors.

"Yes, definitely in his mouth."

Bing came out of the carrier very easily. He seemed disorientated, but clearly in pain. Without instruction, I held on to him so he couldn't move, knowing Dr Stevens is going to have to look in his mouth. The mouth that houses the teeth that scarred the poor Doctor for life.

Carefully, oh so carefully, Dr Stevens opened Bing's mouth and shone a tiny torch inside, knowing that he had a duty of care to this savage animal. Bing allowed him to look, but only for a few seconds before pulling away.

"He's been stung on the back of his tongue," Dr Stevens said, removing his gloves. "It's swollen, which is why he's struggling to breathe, but there are no signs of an allergic reaction. It won't get any worse than this. I can give him something for the pain, to see if that helps to relax him a little. But in a few hours, tomorrow morning at the latest, he'll be back to normal."

"Oh, thank you," I smiled. "That's such a relief. When he was hunched over and struggling to breathe, I really panicked."

"Cats are notorious for getting stung by wasps and bees. Mostly wasps. Bees have the sense to fly away. Wasps fight back and then, well, this happens. And always this time of year too when the weather is changing."

I watch as Dr Stevens prepares a small injection that would hopefully give Bing some comfort.

"Well, thank you so much for seeing us. I know he isn't your favourite patient."

"I can't deny that Bing and I haven't always seen eye to eye, but you never know, we might be best friends one day." He turned around with the needle ready. "Before that day comes though, do you want to hold him down again? Just in case."

19

Dr Stevens advised that it would be best to keep an eye on Bing overnight, and try not to leave him on his own for the first few hours of getting home. As Zack was away for the evening, I had no one to watch Bing for me so my last minute sprint around the shopping centre for holiday bargains turned in to browsing the Dorothy Perkins website to see what I could get delivered for next day collection at my local store. There was very little available. Holiday season was nearly over. Unless I can shrink myself to a size 6 or grow to a size 20, I won't be having much luck with online shopping.

I'd called Zack to fill him in on tonight's drama whilst driving home from the vets.

"Is he alright? Does he need to stay there overnight?" the worry in his voice was so paternal.

"He is fine, he's on the back seat in his carrier growling to himself, so no different to normal really," I sighed. "So it looks like I can't go shopping now. I'll have to go on this posh holiday with my old raggy clothes and out of date bikinis. I hope they still fit."

"Don't you be popping out in front of my Dad, his heart wouldn't be able to cope."

"Ha-ha, they're not that bad actually. It was just an excuse to keep myself busy whilst you were otherwise engaged. Have you got much left to do?"

"No, I'm pretty much done now. I have my holiday gear in a separate bag and all my other stuff packed in boxes ready to take over all the space in your spare room. There's a load of stuff that needs to go to the tip, but Harry is happy for me to leave that until after we get back from the holiday." Harry, his roommate, was thrilled at the prospect of having the place to himself. There was hint that he wanted to move his own girlfriend in, so it looks like everyone is making major relationship changes. "So, we were going to have a few drinks but I can come straight back if you like?"

"No don't be daft, I'll call Sarah and see what she's up to. See if she fancies calling up for a coffee."

"Are you sure?"

"Yes, yes, have your lad's night. Play Xbox, drink beer and light some campfires or something. I'll call her when I get home."

As Bing stumbled out of his carrier, he ran into the living room and onto the sheepskin rug by the fire, curling up into a ball. I brought his food and water to him so he didn't need to go too far if he woke up hungry or thirsty, and then settled myself at the kitchen table to call Sarah. It rang several times before she picked up.

"Hello?"

"Hey, are you busy?"

"Erm, no I'm just chilling. What's up? Aren't you supposed to be shopping?"

"Well, that plan died when Bing decided to chomp on a wasp. A trip to the vets and a hefty bill later, I'm in on my own for the evening."

"Aw no! Is Bing ok?"

"Yeah, he's fine. He'll sleep it off. I was wondering if you wanted to call over for a coffee. Help me to babysit the patient."

"Oh, well actually," she hesitated. "I just wanted a quiet night tonight. Do you mind?"

"Of course not, it's last minute. Blame Bing. Are you feeling ok?"

"Yeah fine, just had a busy day at work so I'm having a Netflix evening."

"How's the dating app going?"

"It's quiet on the dating front, I'm getting bored of that app to be honest. Have you started packing for your holiday yet? One week to go, eek!"

"Not packed yet, plenty of time for that. What do you mean you're getting bored? Just keep swiping, it's fun even if you don't find a date. Has anyone asked you out lately?"

"No, well, yes but no," she stuttered. "I don't know."

"What's going on?"

"What do you mean?"

"You sound all… flustered. Have you been chatting to any guys?"

"Well, I have, and I haven't." I could tell she was biting her lip.

"That makes a lot of sense. Are you alright?"

"I'm fine, honestly, just had a long day and think I'm getting a headache. I'm sorry, I'm being really poop tonight."

"Don't worry, I'll leave you to rest and we'll chat later."

"Call me in a few days and I'm sure I'll be feeling better. And we can arrange when you're bringing Bing over."

"Sounds like a plan. Speak soon."

She must be feeling off, it's not like her not to want to chat, but whether she is bored of the app or not, I'm not done with her blind dates yet. There are more disasters to be had, mwahaha.

Well, if no one is available to hang out this evening, I guess there is only one thing that must be done, sooner than later before I get into bother for not announcing it to the world. I picked up my phone and prepared myself with some calm, deep breaths.

"Well, this is a surprise!"

"Hello Mum," I rolled my eyes, grateful she couldn't see me. "How are you?"

"Just hang on, I need to sit down. My daughter is calling me without me needing to leave twenty missed calls. Be careful, Jen. My heart is not what it used to be."

"You're hilarious."

"Ok, I'm sat down, what's up?"

"Why would there be anything up?"

"Because the last time you called me out of the blue, you were at the airport after your trip to Zante and…"

"Yes, yes, we all remember, thank you." I didn't need to be reminded of that. "Can't a girl just call up her mother to chat?" I could sense her raising her eyebrows at me. "Ok, I have some news"

"Oh? You and Zack haven't broken up have you? You'll never get another man like him. I'll tell you now, he is a rare find. Kind, caring, tall, handsome, and those cheekbones…"

"When you've quite done perving over my boyfriend, I'll tell you my news."

"Ok, ok," she cleared her throat. "Go on then, what's your news?"

"Zack is going to move in with me."

Silence.

"Mum?"

"Sorry, I just wasn't expecting that. I never thought… I never imagined…," she went quiet once more. "That's wonderful."

"Wow," I was stunned. "Thanks. So, you're happy?"

I remember when Andrew announced he and Liz were moving in together. My mum was so happy, she cried. She was so happy that one of her children was settling down. Is she going to cry now? I don't think I've ever made her cry. Well, not happy tears.

"Happy? I'm over the moon! You need a housewarming party," and here we go. I should have text her. "We should have a celebration, after your holiday, I'll make sure all the family know. Are you going to stay there though? It would be nicer to buy somewhere new together. Start afresh. Definitely a party. There'll need to be a vegan choice though, for your brother, I'll sort that. Are you going to redecorate? Maybe get rid of that cat too…"

"Ok, mother, breathe. I was just letting you know the good news. I have to go, Bing needs me."

"Can you send me a guest list?"

"I'll get right on that, goodbye!"

I need a glass of wine.

20

Five days, four hours and thirty-seven minutes until the plane sets off to Crete. Not that I'm counting. Not that I am so excited I could burst but also extremely nervous I could cry. This is my first holiday abroad with my boyfriend, and I'm going with his parents. His parents that I barely know. Who does this? First holidays should be about fondling on the plane, having sex as soon as we get to the hotel, going to the all you can eat buffet, having sex back at the room, wandering down to the beach, having sex in the sea. I'm not sure his parents would appreciate all the sex, especially when we should be doing it in every room like horny teenagers let loose on their own for the first time.

Zack was ready to move all his things in, which we were waiting until after the holiday to do so. I had spent the weekend having a clear out of my own, making way for his things in my wardrobe. He had suggested turning the bigger spare room into a walk-in wardrobe for us, giving us more room in the bedroom, but I had planned on giving him that room as a moving in gift. He could do with an office room for his computer. He often gets the chance to work from home, so it made sense to have his own space. He's moving into *my* house, I don't want him to feel as though he's getting in the way. However, now the idea of a walk-in wardrobe was floating around in my mind, I was envisaging walking into a brightly lit, beige carpeted, spotlight filled ceiling, mirror covered walls with wardrobe space and shoe racks hidden behind them. Maybe he could have the box room instead… although I'm not mentally prepared enough to go through the mess that is the box room.

It was almost eight o'clock. Almost time to call Sarah to plan bringing Bing over. I actually wanted to find out what was going on the other night so had told her to give me a time she was definitely free to chat. She seemed evasive, like she was holding back from me, so I wanted to know what was going on.

She picked up the phone after the first ring.

"Hello!" she sounded her usual happy self. "Five days to go, eek! I bet you're so giddy now and driving everyone mad."

"My tummy doesn't know whether it is excited or nervous," I said. "I barely know his parents and now I'm going to spend fourteen days with them. I've only just felt comfortable enough to fart in front of Zack, now I need to hold it all in for two weeks."

"How much are you farting these days?"

"You know what I mean, I can't embarrass myself in front of them. I don't even know if they know he's moving in with me. I don't know if he's told them and it'll be just like me to slip up and give it away somehow."

"Don't worry about it, you're both grown ups, you're allowed to live together in sin. No one bats an eyelid anymore. Just relax, be yourself, don't fart and you'll be fine."

"I'll try. Anyway, we won't be clung to them for the entire holiday. They said as long as we're together for some evening meals we can do what we like. I guess it's their holiday too so they'll want to do their own thing."

"Exactly, stop stressing. Just think about how you'll be sunning it up for two weeks with your office hunk. No work, no Brexit constantly on the news, just you and him for fourteen sunny days. And if you get a little bit worried, just give me a call. You know I'm here if you need to rant about anything."

"I think I will do," knowing that my best friend is only a phone call away will help me to relax. "Speaking about phone calls, are you ok after the other night? You sounded a bit off."

"Oh yes, it was nothing."

"It sounded like you were having issues with the dating app. Is everything ok? I don't mind if you delete it, don't keep it or my sake if it's getting you down."

"It's not that, I have been chatting to a guy… I think I like him, but it's too soon to say anything yet."

"Ooo, so there is a guy? Tell me more!" I squirmed in my seat, waiting for some good gossip, but Sarah was hesitating.

"It's too soon, I don't want to jinx anything. We met by chance one evening and it was great. We chatted for hours and we text every day. I'll fill you in after your holiday. We can meet up and I'll tell you all the juicy gossip you're sat on the edge of your seat waiting for."

I quietly sat back in my chair, still giddy that Sarah could finally have met someone perfect. Someone decent. Someone who she likes so much she doesn't even want to risk jinxing anything.

"Ok, ok, just promise me you will tell me *everything* when I get back?"

"I promise," she said. "I'll tell you all about him and how we met."

"Good," I was satisfied, knowing that my friend was happy. "So, when can I bring Bing around to you? We fly Thursday morning, so I can call around on Wednesday evening if that's alright?"

"Yes, I'll be free then. I'm meeting, erm, my friend Tuesday night for tea so Wednesday is great, just promise me you won't try and interrogate me until after your holiday. Don't be sniffing around looking for clues."

"I don't know what you mean, just ignore the webcam I attach around Bing's neck won't you?"

"Ha, ha. Very funny. Have you packed yet?"

We chatted for the next twenty minutes and I was satisfied that the other night was just a blip and there was nothing wrong with Sarah. We all have those off days. I usually did when it was her leaving me on my own to go on holiday to some exotic land. The tables have turned, I guess.

Now she was staying at home whilst her best friend was jetting off. At least she would have Bing for company. If that can be considered a good thing.

21

Three days, one hour and twelve minutes until take off.

"So, tell me again about the villa," I snuggled into Zacks nook. "What does it look like? Where abouts is it? How many bedrooms did you say there were?" We were both finally on annual leave from work and were spending our Monday morning in bed. Our morning was certainly glorious as Bing had been banished from the bedroom.

"There's nothing to tell, really. It's a villa. A very nice villa, but they're all the same," he said, casually. "It has four bedrooms, so when you're sick of me you can kick me out. All en-suites. Two living room areas. A kitchen with a dining area. An outdoor cooking area with dining space. There's a pool in the gym, as well as the shared one outside."

"So, it's not a villa then, it's a mansion. Just how rich are your parents?"

"Ha! Ok, it's pretty big I guess. It sits on a piece a land about a mile away from the sea and shares the outdoor pool with a neighbouring villa which is owned by some family friends. They might be there too, this time of year, with their daughter. My parents usually invite them over a lot to eat with us."

"I won't have to entertain the daughter will I?" I can see it now, some bored, pain in the arse teenager that gets pushed on to me.

"Chloe is capable of entertaining herself by now. She's twenty-one."

"Oh?" Alarm bells began to ring. "How well do you know her?"

"I've known her all her life. Our parents are very close. She's cool, very funny. I think you'll get on."

"Oh good," I rolled my eyes, thinking back to Sarah's theory of the twenty-something girls. "Yes, I'm sure we will."

I rolled over away from him, not wanting to show him the worry on my face. I've just washed all my bikinis, but I can't be seen in a bikini with someone nearly ten years younger than me. I'll have to walk around all day with my arms up in the air, just to make sure my boobs are being pulled in the right way. Could I get away with wearing a burkini?

"Hey, why have you turned away?" Zack spooned into me, a perfect fit, making me smile and relax. Suddenly, Bing let out a howl at the bedroom door.

"He'll be hungry," I moaned. "We should get up."

Zack pulled me tightly, his reluctance to get out of bed evident judging by the pressure I was suddenly feeling in my back.

"Do we have to? A few more minutes."

Bing wailed louder.

"I think we have to," I threw back the duvet, walking naked to my dressing gown which was left on the floor leaving me no choice but to bend over for it, giving Zack an X-rated view.

"You tease." He rolled back over to his side of the bed whilst I saw to the cat that was clearly dying of hunger as he'd not been fed for twelve hours.

Bing followed me downstairs, attached to my leg like a magnet, and he did not shut up meowing until I had given him some food. I'll need to warn Sarah that he can get hangry. If he damages any of her new furniture out of some kind of protest, he will be living in my shed.

I sent Sarah a message:

"Possibly sharing my holiday with a 20something… send me words of encouragement to stop me binning my bikinis! Xx"

I wonder if it's too late to book a holiday to Alaska…

"You are fabulous! Gorgeous! Boobs never looked better! You make those Victoria's Secret models look like they've chomped on too many burgers! Xxxxx"

"A bit too far… but nice try. You looking forward to your date? I mean… seeing your friend ;) Xx"

"I am, I'm all nervous! Can't decide what to wear. Might need to go shopping after work X"

I'd love a shopping trip, seeing as though Bing ruined my last chance after he decided to munch on a wasp.

"Can I come too? I can help you find something whilst perusing the holiday section :) Xx"

She didn't reply instantly, so I popped the kettle on and set up two cups. I undid my dressing gown, looking down at my body. I was slumped forward which wasn't a flattering look, my belly all rolled up and ancient boobs sat atop the flab. I stood up straight, pushing my chest out, releasing them from their cushioned seats so they were standing alone. They still didn't look great though. I blew some cold air on them, making them look a little bit perkier. Hmm, not bad. Still got it. I just need to make sure I walk around with my chest pushed out the whole holiday and… oh shit.

I quickly closed my dressing gown, turning away from the Chinese Hermes delivery guy who was staring at me, wide eyed, through the kitchen window.

"Oh, bugger!"

"What's happened?" Zack rushed into the kitchen, looking around.

"Oh, I just showed off the goods to Fred. Full frontal everything. Nothing major." My face burned as I turned back to see Fred waving a parcel, unable to speak any words. Zack went to the back door and signed for it.

"I've heard of tipping delivery guys but, I think he got more than he deserved. This parcel isn't even for you, it's for next door. What the hell do you offer when it's for you?" he couldn't hold in his laughter, as much as he tried.

"Sod off and make the drinks. I'm off for a shower."

I picked up my phone and read Sarah's delayed reply.

"I'm just going to go straight from work, another time yeah? Love you Xx"

Why doesn't she want me to go shopping with her?

22

One day to go.

This time tomorrow, we will be on our merry way to beautiful, exotic, dreamland Crete. My suitcase was packed, my passport was in my bag, my carry on bag was ready, I was waxed everywhere I needed to be. I was in absolute holiday mode. Nothing could bring me down today. Not the rain lashing down outside, not the empty fridge meaning there was nothing to eat and not even the horrifying memory of flashing Fred everything I had to offer (pre-wax… even worse).

I had bought a new bag of food for Bing and put together a few of his things to make Sarah's home more familiar for him. He was currently in hiding. I made the mistake of getting his carrier from under the stairs and setting it up ready for him to go in… he did not take too kindly to that.

Zack wandered into the kitchen and opened the fridge.

"It's empty," I said.

"We don't even have any milk for a drink," he moaned. "We'll need a coffee in the morning before we go. We need to set off at five o'clock."

"Say what now?" I stopped in my tracks.

"We need to set off at five o'clock." He looked at me as though I should have been aware of this traumatic news. "The flight is at eight, it takes roughly forty-five minutes to get to the airport. I doubt there'll be traffic at that time, but I need to check my car into their carpark as soon as we get there."

"I thought the flight was at ten?" I'm sure that was the time we had booked.

"We looked at a few flights, didn't we?" Did we? "And we decided to go with the earlier one so we'd have more time in Crete." I vaguely recall a conversation about flights, but I don't remember agreeing to such a satanic wake up time. Zack pulled out his phone and started scrolling. "Here, see."

He passed me his phone so I could look at the flight details on his email. Sure enough, we had booked the eight o'clock flight. Dammit. Day one of my holiday and I'll be up before the birds. I was suddenly calculating times in my head. I'd planned on a morning shower, but if we're leaving here at five, I'd need to get up at four. Actually, no, half three, because I'll need to make sure I pack my hair straighteners when they've cooled down. I can't pack them hot. Half three? Who gets up at half three?

I was flapping. Panicking. I'd planned it all out but now I couldn't decide what to do.

"Are you alright?" Zack stared at me.

"I'm just trying to work things out, don't you worry. Silly girly preparation stuff."

"Ok, well, you ponder over girly stuff, I'm going to pop to the shop for a pint of milk and grab us a pizza for tea. Unless you want to order a takeaway tonight?"

Hmm, a takeaway tonight means a potentially irritable bowel situation on the plane tomorrow.

"Just grab a pizza, that'll do."

He kissed me as he grabbed his keys and said he wouldn't be long.

I decided it would be best to have a shower tonight so I could get up at a less evil hour tomorrow. It just meant I would need to take Bing over to Sarah's a little earlier. I checked the time, she should be at work so I could just take him over now. I have a spare key, she wouldn't mind.

I dialled her number, which I knew off by heart, but there was no answer. I wandered around the kitchen and tried again, still no answer. She must be in a meeting. I decided to send her a message.

"Hey! Change of plan, I'm going to bring Bing over at lunch time. I'll leave him in your kitchen with food and water (did you set up that litter box?) if not, I'll find it and do it. Ciaooo Xx"

I opened the fridge, but the food fairy still hadn't delivered anything for me to eat. The cupboards were bare, unless I fancied a tin of peas and carrots. Zack might need to bring something back for lunch as well as tea. I sent him a message to bring back enough food for the day and about the change of plans for Bing.

When I was dressed, and in no danger of flashing anyone else today, I made sure all of Bing's things were in my car. All that was left to do now, was grab the escape artist. I made sure my arms and legs were covered to protect myself from his claws.

"Oh Biiiiing. Bingy Bing." I crept around the hall and poked my head into the lounge. Nothing. "Come on Bing, come on." Nothing. "Dreamies." Like the poof of a genie at the rub of a lamp, Bing apparated onto the armchair, ears pointing up and tail fluffed. I held out my hand, revealing two of his tasty treats. But Bing was not so dumb.

I stepped back with the Dreamies still in my hand, trying to tempt him my way, but he stayed put. He blinked, whiskers flared, and slowly turned around so his back was facing me. I didn't have time to mess about. I put the treats in my pocket and lunged forward, grabbing him unexpectedly and risking certain death by a thousand scratches by quickly shoving him in the carrier.

"There we go," I said, triumphantly. "That wasn't so bad, was it?"

My car rolled down Sarah's driveway just after twelve. I smiled at her house, admiring how far my friend had come this year. From seeing her looking so broken thanks to Max the Wanker, she was a born again independent woman. And now, my friend was back on the dating scene and had found someone she liked. I was disappointed that she hadn't met him on the app, but I still couldn't wait to hear all the gory details.

Bing grumbled from the backseat.

"Ok, ok. We're going."

I fumbled with the keys and eventually found myself in the kitchen. There were two empty dishes on the floor by the fridge and an empty litter tray by the front door, the bag of gravel sitting inside it. I decided to leave the happy cat inside his carrier until I had everything ready for him so I could make my exit, not needing to look at his bemused face for longer than I needed to. I thought I heard something above me, creaking floorboards, but in my haste, I didn't really think about it. Houses make noise. I had asked Sarah whether it was a good idea buying such an old house.

"Not all old houses are haunted," she reassured me. "Walls crack and floorboards creak, it happens."

I wasn't entirely convinced then, and I still wasn't now. As long as I ignored the creaking, and the footsteps, and whatever was approaching the door to the kitchen, my heart was pounding with fear and I grabbed the nearest object I could find.

"A spatula? Really?" Sarah stepped into the kitchen and closed the door behind her. "You almost gave me a heart attack, I thought someone had broken in."

"Right back at ya sista," I put the spatula back on the counter. "What are you doing here? Where's your car?"

"I left it in town, I was going to pick it up later."

"Ah yes, the date." I looked at my friend who was still fastening her dressing gown and flattening her bed head. Or trying to, at least. That hair was the sign of a good night. "The bed got christened last night then?"

She blushed.

"Well, erm…"

"It's ok, it's ok," I held up my hands. "We're saving all the juicy gossip for when I'm back. I won't push you for details. Did you get my message?"

"No," her eyes darted to the door, hearing the footsteps making their way from the bedroom. "Just leave Bing's things and I'll…"

The door opened.

There he stood.

Dan.

23

I was at a loss for words. Dan. My Dan. My very own ex-friend-with-benefits. So, he was the guy she had been seeing. The one she liked and had been texting every day since they had their first date. She couldn't tell me. My best friend couldn't tell me that she was going to be meeting up with Dan. After everything, she couldn't trust me.

Thoughts and words were flying around inside my head, not making any sense. I looked down at Bing in his carrier. It was too late to take him home and find somewhere else for him to stay for the next two weeks. I didn't look at Sarah. I couldn't.

"He's eaten," I pointed at Bing. "Don't let him make you think he's dying of hunger. He will be lying." I picked up his bag of food and toys and placed them on Sarah's table. "His things are in there. They might make him a bit more comfortable."

"Jenny…"

"I have to go, I have some things still to pack. I'll call you when I'm home and arrange picking him up."

"Jenny…" I heard Dan's voice as I turned around and made my way out the door, followed closely by a frantic

Sarah who held my car door, preventing me from shutting it and driving away as quickly as possible.

"I'm sorry," she said, tears forming in her panicked eyes. "I was going to tell you when you got back. I didn't know where this would head. If it would even head anywhere."

"I need to go, Sarah. We'll talk after my holiday, like we originally planned." I held on to the steering wheel, too scared to look at her in case I started to cry too.

"Look, I get that it's weird and I can kind of understand why you'd be jealous, but…"

"Jealous?" I cut her off. "You think I'm jealous? Sarah, Dan can do whatever the hell he likes. *You* can do what you like. You and he can do whatever you like. I don't care that you and he are together."

"Then what's the problem?" Her panic switched to confusion.

"The problem is, after everything we have been through, not just the last twelve months, *everything*, you couldn't pick up the phone and tell me you were going on a date with Dan."

"I didn't know how you'd react," she admitted.

"And that's the problem. You didn't want to find out how I might react. You just went ahead even though you thought I would be mad. *That* is the problem."

"I'm sorry." It was her turn to be at a loss for words. Dan appeared at the doorway.

"I need to go. I'll see you in a couple of weeks."

Sarah stepped back and allowed me to shut the car door. I pulled away, not wanting to look at either of them.

24

I didn't even notice my brother's car parked outside my house. My head was spinning with thoughts by the time I got home a few hours later. I needed to clear my head so had driven to Ogden Reservoir where I knew it would be peaceful at this time of day.

I tried picturing Sarah and Dan together. They would make a good couple. I have known them both for a long time. Dan has matured over the years and from looking at his dating app profile, he was ready for love. If he was going to find the right kind of girl anywhere who would be a partner as well as a best friend, it was Sarah. She had learned from mistakes with Max The Wanker, her barriers might have been up with other dates, but she would know what she was getting with Dan as I had spoken about him for years. He could be trusted, unless he was sent to buy bedroom furniture. Maybe they spent the night at Sarah's house because I had told her all about the waterbed horrors.

Regardless of poor mattress choices, I know they will be a strong couple, so why was I so angry?

I had wandered around the reservoir, ignoring the rain clouds above threatening to unleash on me, and thought about all Sarah and I had been through. The dramas of shitty boyfriends, the horrors of the university hangovers, the holiday to Zante in 2010. We were best friends, maybe even soul mates, so why couldn't she speak to me first? Why couldn't she tell me they were meeting up for a date? Just… why couldn't she talk to me?

Zack met me in the hallway as I walked through the door.

"Where've you been? I was getting worried."

I could see the worry in his eyes as he pulled me close enough to feel his heart beating.

"I was just hanging out with Sarah, lost track of time," I lied. Great, now I was the dishonest one. On my walk, I had wondered about telling Zack why I'd had a fallout with Sarah. Would he take it the wrong way and think I had feelings for Dan? Or would he understand that I felt betrayed? I didn't want to be the hypocrite and keep things from him. "Actually, I had a thing with Sarah…"

"Is she back? Is she still in one piece?" Andrews voice shouted from the living room. Did Zack call in the cavalry to search for me?

"Hey," I walked into the room. "What are you doing here?"

"Liz found my stash of sausage rolls in the garage and threw me out."

"What?!" I dropped my bag to the floor at his announcement. "Are you being serious? Oh, that bloody woman…"

"I'm kidding! Calm down. I installed an integrated fridge in one of the garage units, so she'll never find out," he winked. "But if you have any bacon I'd be up for a butty. And sausages. And burgers. Anything."

Zack laughed.

"The poor guy, he's lacking good, decent protein. Why don't we order something in?"

"Actually, I can't stick around too long," he checked his phone. "Liz is needing me back to help get the kids fed, bathed and in bed. But if I leave now, I'll be able to nip to the shop and restock my fridge."

He stood up and put on his organic cotton jacket to go with his hemp t-shirt. I was surprised to see his trousers weren't made out of dock leaves and his shoes weren't coconut shells.

"You never answered my question," I said. "What are you doing here?"

"I was just on my way back from a conference in Leeds and thought I'd call in. Zack and I were just catching up, talking sports, debating the best way to build a fire, typical man stuff."

"Ok, ok. Go back to your mud hut and eat your hummus. We'll be tucking into a meat feast pizza as soon as you're gone."

He playfully punched my arm and then pulled me in for a hug goodbye.

"Have a great holiday," he pulled back. "Zack was telling me about the villa. It sounds awesome! A lot better than that place you stayed in Zante with the…"

"Ok! Goodbye Andrew, it's been a pleasure."

"See you soon bud," he said to Zack as I forcefully but nicely shoved him out the door before he could say anymore.

"That was random," I said. "I can't remember the last time my brother was at my house. What was he really up to?"

"He was just passing, like he said. So, we had a chat over a coffee. Are you hungry? I'll go put some food in the oven. Then it's an early night." He kissed me on the head and made his way to the kitchen.

I pulled my phone out of my bag and there were two missed calls and a message from Sarah.

"Please forgive me. I did a shitty thing. You didn't deserve that. Call me. I'll always be here X"

I put my phone away. I wasn't ready to call her just yet.

25

Our taxi from the airport to the villa took a couple of hours. I should have been bored, a thirty-minute taxi through Halifax is bad enough, but Crete was the most beautiful place I had ever seen. And that includes the inside of the Cadbury factory. Free chocolate vs clear blue skies, even clearer seas and an air-conditioned taxi keeping us cool from the thirty-degree heat that almost melted me as I stepped off the plane... Crete wins without a doubt. I didn't even need my little fan.

The taxi was a shock to the system too. Back home, you would usually be in a ten year old Nissan or Toyota (if you were lucky) but our ride to Zacks parent's villa was in a brand new Mercedes. I worried about the cost with being in such a snazzy car but looking around at the taxis passing on the other side of the road, they were all brand new cars as well. Not a rust bucket on wheels in sight. Zack's parents insisted on paying for our ride as it was too late to book a coach transfer. I dread to think what it might come to.

"This is Agios Nikolaos," Zack said as we drove through a busy town. "We're nearly there now." He looked around in wonder at the place he had spent many summers growing up.

There were streets full of shops and restaurants. The marina was full of yachts and there was an actual cruise ship parked up too! I spied all the touristy shops full of nick knacks and tat. I love those shops. They all sell the same stuff for the same price, but I still feel the need to go in and buy something I would never buy at home. Like a ceramic Hercules which I am sure every Cretan has in their home.

"Could we come back and do some shopping?" I asked.

"Of course! We can do whatever we like. We have two whole weeks here." He reached for my hand. "There will be plenty of time for shopping."

The taxi wove down narrow roads and out of the town. We passed huge, five star hotels and eventually drove down a long driveway with a few villas dotted about. They were all painted white with blue shutters, and perfect manicured lawns out front with Greek pots decorating the doorways. 'Villa' was a very modest term for these mansions, although I did not say that to Zack.

"And we're here!" Zack squeezed my hand before getting out of the taxi. The driver was already at the boot getting our cases out for us.

"Hello, travellers!" Alistair came out of the palace before us, looking tiny in comparison, with his arms open wide to greet his son and me. "How was the flight? Was there a long wait for your suitcases? I do hope there wasn't any traffic. Oh, let me pay for the taxi." He finally stopped to take a breath whilst moving his sunglasses to the top of his pink head. I didn't see how much he paid, but there was no change handed back to him which is was not fazed by. Even if I was owed fifty pence, I would want my change.

"Where's Mum?" Zack asked.

"She's just having a siesta, she's been out in the garden all morning, seeing to the flowers. Tired the poor old girl out." He picked up my suitcase. "Don't tell her I called her that." He winked and led us both inside.

The entrance hall could have been a room on its own. In fact, I initially thought I was walking into the sitting room as there were two large sofas and a coffee table. He took us to the bottom of the stairs in the far corner and plonked down my case.

"I'll let Zack give you the official tour, I have to get back to Stan. He's got the football on at his place and, whilst the ladies are having their afternoon naps, we aren't getting any complaints," he chuckled. "I will see you two kids later on."

He put his sunglasses back on and sauntered through another door and out of sight.

"Who's Stan?"

"Stan and Beverley, my parent's friends who own the villa next door. They'll be here with their daughter Chloe." He picked up our suitcases. "Come on, I'll race you upstairs."

"Woah, slow down," I grabbed his arm. "Won't we wake your mum?" I didn't want to annoy her on my first day here. She should at least get to know me before she hates me.

"Not a chance, their room is in the opposite direction to ours."

Looking up to the landing, I felt like I was in *Downton Abbey* again. I don't think I could even call it a landing. It was more like a gallery with a huge window in the tall ceiling, allowing the sun to beam down the stairs. I followed my giddy boyfriend to the top and then down the west wing and through a door, expecting David Bowie to pop out in his inappropriate tight trousers, dancing and singing with a bunch of gremlins.

"Well, this just won't do." I shook my head at the ridiculously sized room. "It's not even remotely big enough for the two of us," I said as I sat on the king size bed looking up to the double doors which led out to a balcony. There were two double wardrobes and a grey patterned chair in the corner next to a desk and some shelves filled with books. If I were to wear a pedometer and walk once around the room, I am pretty sure I would hit the recommended daily step count.

"Not big enough?"

"Nope, sorry, you'll need to sleep somewhere else."

He put the cases down in front of the wardrobes and came over to me, pushing me down on the bed and climbing on top.

"You would kick me out of my own room?" He nuzzled at my neck, kissing me in the right place.

"Absolutely. You'd need to sleep in the servant's quarters under the stairs."

His lips moved up my neck and to my lips. It feels like ages since we were intimate. It was more like two days, but still, long enough.

"I'll be right back." He kissed me once more and then bounced back off the bed and through another door.

"Where does that door lead to? Cinema? Recording studio?"

"Just the en-suite, nothing that exciting," he smiled and closed the door. I may never want to leave this place.

I got up and walked to the balcony. Clicking the latch, I slid open the doors and let the sun hit my face for a moment. It didn't feel as uncomfortable as Rome. In Rome, I knew I would be walking around for hours and hours in the heat, but here, there is a pool at my disposal.

Stepping forward, I looked around and saw a few villas dotted around. There was no one around, maybe everyone was having an afternoon snooze. I glanced down at the pool and smiled to myself. It didn't matter that it was shared with Alistair and Miranda's friends. It was huge, and there were a dozen sunbeds around it as well as couches and umbrellas for shade. It was heaven. My tan will be amazeballs after this. Maybe I could be brave and wear one of my bikinis after all.

Then again.

Maybe I won't.

My eyes nearly fell out of my head as I spotted the girl I assumed was Chloe, the daughter. The twenty-something. A twenty-something with the body of a Victoria Secret model and breasts perky enough to poke your eye out, clearly displayed in her barely-there bikini. I'm only thirty-one, and I've never had children, but I feel like I should be wearing a burkini instead of a bikini. This was supposed to be a relaxing holiday, but I can't compete with her.

Two arms came from behind and pulled me close.

"Enjoying the view?" Zack asked.

Not as much as he probably is. How many summers has he spent here with her looking like that? There's a ten year age gap, but still, summer loving and all that.

"It's amazing," I looked back up to the actual scenic view. "Although I am disappointed I can't see the sea. I won't be leaving a good review on Trip Advisor."

"It's on the other side," his hands were wandering. "I'll show you later."

"Is that Chloe?" I had to ask. Probably not my smartest move averting his eyes to that imagery whilst he fondles my ancient body.

"It is," he glanced down for a second to check before returning his attention to me.

"Does she always dress like that?"

"Only when her parents aren't looking, they're quite conservative." His hand found my bra, which he undid in record time. "Come on, let's get you unpacked."

"We are so glad you're here!" Miranda said, clinking my glass of wine. Alistair had just cooked a delicious tea. I was conscious of trying not to eat too much, worried I will gain too much weight and look like a beached whale, but the more wine Zack's mum poured for me, the less I cared.

"It is such a beautiful house," I exclaimed. "I swear, I almost got lost when I nipped up to the bathroom."

Zack and his parents laughed. He held on to my hand. He seemed different. Maybe it was the change of environment, maybe he was just glad to be on holiday, but he seemed really content.

"I just wish I'd been awake to greet you." She playfully slapped her husband's arm. "You should have woken me up."

"Oh, I know better than that my love," he leaned forward and kissed her cheek.

"Don't worry it's fine, Zack had to give me a tour anyway." And see that I was sufficiently satisfied atop every piece of furniture in our room.

"Well," she gulped the last of her wine, her eyes seeming heavy. "We'll leave you kids to it for a few days. We won't get in your way. Do what you like, but we will be having a big meal here one night this week along with next door so I hope you'll join us for that."

"Of course," I grinned. I love Miranda. If this were my mother, she would have a military planned itinerary for us, with something on every day and no chance of alone time. "We can help out."

"Not at all, once that barbecue is lit, Beverley and I are banished from the cooking area. All we need to do is pick out the wine."

"That seems like a serious job, I am willing to help."

"I'm glad to hear it." She squeezed my arm. I want her to adopt me.

"Well, my dear," Alistair piped up, placing his empty glass on the table. "That's todays wine allowance used up. Shall we call it a night?"

"I think we should."

They stood up and I felt obliged to do the same, along with Zack. They bid us goodnight, instructing us to enjoy our evening and to leave the used glasses out to be cleaned away in the morning.

"Fancy a skinny dip?" Zack whispered, as soon as his parents were out of earshot.

"What's gotten into you?" I blushed. "You're never usually this daring. How much wine have you had?"

"Not a lot, I hate the stuff. Come on, no one will see."

And so, filled up on expensive wine and clearly suffering some form of heatstroke to be even remotely willing to do this… I stripped down to my birthday suit, and my thirty-one-year-old boobs and I joined my naked boyfriend for a quick dip in the pool. I do hope this water has a self-cleaning function after our antics…

As we climbed into bed, I checked my phone and there was a message from Sarah. No words, just a photo of Bing, curled up asleep in her new armchair.

"Have you spoke to her yet?" Zack asked.

"No." I put my phone on the side table and laid down in bed.

"Just let things cool down whilst you're here. Try and talk to her when we get home."

I realise I'll have to talk to her at some point, she has my cat… but what on earth would I say to her? I don't need to think about it yet. I have two weeks of living in paradise ahead of me. Whether or not my relationship with Sarah can be saved is a problem for another time. I wasn't important enough for her to tell me something as little with going on a date with my ex-friend-with-benefits, so why should I fret now?

It was a relief telling Zack on the plane. I'm so glad he understood why I was upset, but he says it will all blow over soon enough. I do hope so. I need to brag that I just swam naked in my boyfriend's parent's pool and had sex on a sun lounger, and there is only one person in my life who would appreciate such gossip. Particularly after the incident in Zante…

26

It was a very bad idea walking the short distance into Agios Nikolaos. The sun was hot hot hot and my feet were now dead dead dead. Once in the centre of the town, we walked over a bridge which ran over a river of sea which lead to a small lake surrounded by restaurants and a rocky hill side with various religious carvings. And cats. Lots of cats that clearly live outside yet are much friendlier than Bing. You could just make out the fish sitting in the shade of the bridge, almost teasing me to join them. It was only ten o'clock, but it was scorching. We stopped at one of the restaurants for a break and a waiter told me that locals believed the lake to be bottomless and that one of the Greek Goddesses used to bathe in it at night. Never mind waiting until night-time when the sun has gone down, I want to get in there now.

We rehydrated ourselves on freshly squeezed orange juice and rested our feet before setting off again and taking in more of the town. The shops were so cute, one actually led down into a cave where a little old Greek man was selling his handmade wooden souvenirs. Zack had to drag me out of the shop selling handmade jewellery and I had to drag him away from the street vendor selling headphones and other knock off gadgets.

We held hands as we walked past the cruise ship stationed at the marina, a different one to yesterday, and around the coastline all I could see was blue. It was difficult to see where the sky ended and the sea began. After the obligatory loved up selfies with blue backgrounds, we descended further. I could understand why Zack's parents would want their holiday home to be here. It was wonderful.

"Let me know when you're hungry," Zack said as we were sat on a bench watching a man sitting with his legs off the pier, an empty bucket on one side of him and bait on the other as he firmly held his fishing rod. "We can find somewhere to eat. You have a lot of places to pick from."

"I know where I want to eat," I said confidently.

"If you're waiting for Achilles to snag a fish, you could be waiting a while."

Our Greek fisherman was not having much luck.

"Dammit. Well my second option was back near the lake, the restaurant which sits on the sea edge. It looked lovely."

"I've been there, you'll love the pizzas." He stood up and pulled me up with him. "Whenever Chloe was getting sick of her parents bickering at her, we'd come down and grab some food there. It's a great place."

I felt a pang of jealousy hit me right in the gut. I've still not met her yet and already I'm beginning to hate her. I just need to keep reminding myself that he brought me here with him. Even though she would have been here and he could have left me at home, he brought me. I need to stop being silly.

It was just after one o'clock as we arrived at the restaurant, just in time for lunch. The tables were sheltered with a huge canopy so we could enjoy our food without feeling like we were on a grill. There were fans scattered about too blowing warm air onto us, which was still nice.

We both ordered ice water and asked for a few minutes to look over the menu. I looked up at Zack sitting across me. He was reading his menu but glanced up and smiled at me with his mischievous grin.

"What are you thinking?" I flirted with him, tickling his leg with my foot.

"I'm wondering if we could get the pool to ourselves again tonight."

"What did you have in mind?" I leaned in closer, not wanting the neighbouring tables to hear us.

"Oh my god, Zack! Aahhh!" The unmistakeable mating call of a twenty-something girl echoed around the restaurant.

We both looked up and saw Chloe bounding towards us, her twenty abs on show for the whole of Crete to see. Zack was barely able to stand up before she threw her arms around him, her long hair flinging over his shoulders as though claiming its territory. It's ok guys, go ahead, I'll wait. I subconsciously made sure my own top was pulled down over my tummy.

"Hey you," Zack pulled back. "What are you doing down here?"

"Oh, my mum was driving me up the wall," she pulled back the chair next to Zack, putting her shopping bags under the table, and sat down. "She was going on and on about me going back to uni and finishing my law degree. I had to get out." She turned to me and elbowed Zack in the side. "Are you going to introduce us then? Tut, men!" she laughed, "they're so rude, aren't they?"

As Zack made official introductions, I outstretched my hand but she got up from her seat and smothered me with a hug too.

"It is so nice to finally meet you!" she returned to the seat next to Zack. "It's so nice to finally have a girl here too. Not that Zack isn't fun, with the amount of late-night pool parties we had." She winked at him. "Has he made you his Pina Colada yet? He makes such a good cocktail." She rubbed his arm. "We got so wasted last year, do you remember?"

"Vaguely," he laughed, looking uncomfortable.

"My mum was so mad as we'd used all the rum. Hilarious. It was worth the scolding."

They seemed so comfortable in each other's company which was nice, but the idea of them getting drunk and having a pool party of their own made me lose my appetite, even if it was in the past. I had a niggling urge to call Sarah. I need her to tell me it's all ok.

"Have you ordered yet? I'm starving."

"We were just looking over the menu, have you decided yet?" He reached out for my hand, pulling me out of my nightmare daze.

"Erm, no, well actually…"

"We should get a pizza," Chloe cut in. "Get the massive one and share it. It'll be enough for the three of us, it was too much for just us two last year but I reckon we can manage."

"Let's do it, we're on holiday." Zack put his menu down and called the waiter over, ordering the large pepperoni pizza. At least he picked my favourite topping.

An hour later, I should have been in total bliss. Delicious pizza, sexy boyfriend sat opposite me, the never ending sea to my right, but unfortunately there was something on our table demanding all of the attention. If I had a shot of rum for every time she rubbed his arm, I would be mighty tipsy. Why can't she just back off? I get that they've known each other for a long time, but you don't constantly touch someone's boyfriend right in front of them. Was she jealous that he was here with another woman?

"Well, I should go," *it* finally said, standing up. "Do you want any money for the pizza?" She put her hand on Zack's shoulder and I fought every urge not to push her into the sea.

"Nah, don't worry about it," Zack said.

"Ok, laters!" she felt the need to bend down, arse so close to Zack's face he could have kissed it, to pick her bags from the floor and finally leave us alone. So much for a romantic lunch, all I can picture now is her perfect buttocks and thigh gap. She doesn't need to worry about chafing in this heat.

"Are you alright?" he asked. "You've been pretty quiet."

"Oh yeah, it's pretty hot. I can get grumpy if I'm too hot, sorry." It was true, I did get grumpy when too hot, but it was a lie right now. This was supposed to be a relaxing holiday, a first holiday, with my boyfriend. How can I relax if Chloe was going to pop up at every moment? Can't she learn to sod off?

"Well let's head back up, we can get a taxi and have a siesta." Now it was his turn to tease my leg with his foot. He rubbed my hand with his finger, up my arm to my face, pulling me close as he leaned over the table to kiss me. "Sorry about Chloe, she is used to being centre of attention. She probably monopolised our lunch there."

"Just a bit. Not to mention talking none stop about you two having mad summer pool parties."

"Not like our pool party last night, don't think that. She's not interested in me. We've been friends for a long time, ever since our parents bought those villas."

The waiter came by with our bill and Zack pulled out some money.

"I don't mind if you want to walk back up," I lied, "save money on a taxi."

"In this heat? Neither of us will survive. Come on," he grabbed my hand, pulling me up with him. "our bath is big enough for the two of us. No one can interrupt us in there."

27

Day three of our holiday and things are a lot nicer today in terms of privacy. Alistair and Miranda have gone out for the day, and Stan, Beverley and Chloe are out too. The villa and pool are all ours. And with it being private for just the two villas, no one can see us as we fooled around under water. Pool sex was an odd experience. We started out on the lilo and, well, that's how we ended up under water.

"What time is everyone due back?" I asked as I wrapped myself in a towel and positioned myself on a sun lounger under an umbrella for some shade. It was mid-afternoon and near thirty degrees. Definitely time for an afternoon nap.

"I don't know." He pulled one of the loungers up to mine so we could lay together. "Later on tonight I think. Do you want a drink before we snuggle up?" He had been so attentive today. Whether it was to make me feel better for yesterday, I'm not sure. Or had I just forgotten that this was just who he was? Every night before bed, he always asks if I needed anything bringing. One night I had left my phone in the living room. We were already tucked up and falling asleep, but once I realised and was about to get up, he jumped out of bed to get it for me. That's just who he was.

"I'm alright, thanks," I pulled my sunglasses down over my eyes. I was finally feeling like I was on holiday. Zack laid next to me now that our sun loungers were together and pulled me close so we could spoon. "This is so comfy. Can we stay here forever?"

"You won't get any argument from me. This is heaven."

A gentle breeze blew over us. A cricket called out from somewhere in the grass. Zack's breathing got heavier behind me as he began to fall asleep. Otherwise, the silence filled my ears, and I was soon joining Zack in the land of nod.

I was lost in the villa. Each door led me back to the entrance. How do I get out? I could hear laughter through the door to my right. I push it open, expecting to be in the dining room, but I am back in the entrance. I run up the flight of stairs and through our bedroom door, but I am back in the entrance. Help!

"Zack!" I called out. "Where are you? Help!"

"I'm through here!" he laughed, as he shouted from the living room.

I ran forward, pushing the door open, expecting to be back where I started, but I could see the back of the sofa. Finally, I was no longer trapped in a labyrinth. Zacks head was visible, so I walked around to join him, but he was sitting with Chloe. No, he was laid on top of her on the sofa. They were cuddling, kissing...

"What's going on?" I shouted? "What are you doing?"

I woke myself up by calling out. Zack shuffled behind me.

"Are you alright? You jumped pretty hard there. Did you fall over in a dream?"

"Something like that," my towel had slipped down, exposing my cleavage. I was brave enough to wear a bikini today knowing we would be all alone, but I suddenly felt very insecure. "What time is it?" I removed my sunglasses, feeling where they had dug into the side of my head and left an engraving.

"Woah, almost four. We've slept for a while." He yawned as he sat up and stretched. "Oh, hello! When did you get here?"

I looked up to see who he was talking to, like I didn't already know.

"I've been here ages. You two were well out of it!" Chloe was on the sun lounger opposite us, laying on her front and evidently topless. "You were making some funny noises, Jenny," she giggled. "Sounded like you were having a kinky dream."

"I thought you were out all day?" Zack enquired.

"Nah, I couldn't be arsed. I slept in late and was going to come out here but saw you two were, erm, enjoying yourselves," she winked. I was mortified. "So, I hid inside until you fell asleep and came out. Actually," she sat up, pulling her top across her front. "Zack, could you top up the sun cream on my back for me? I don't think I got everywhere, I'd hate to burn."

"Of course," he said, without thinking. I watched as he sat behind her, rubbing factor ten cream into her neck and shoulders. I mean, come on. Factor ten? Why bother? You may as well rub milk into your skin. Why is she doing this?

I pulled my towel over myself and stood up.

"Where are you going, babe?" He asked.

"Just nipping to the bathroom, won't be a tick."

As soon as I got inside, I ran up the stairs, holding back tears. In our room I found my phone. There was another photo from Sarah with a message. This time, Bing was in her kitchen, sprawled on his back in a seemingly mischievous mood.

"Your cat ate my red thong… he's ok. The thong however had a grim ending X"

I laughed out loud, tears filling my eyes. My finger hovered over the 'call' button, but I hesitated. Our first conversation had to be about her and Dan. I didn't want to break our silence with my tears over a silly bit of jealousy. I peeked out the window and down at Zack and Chloe. They were laughing together, their heads close. She playfully pushed him away. In my mind I was 'playfully' pushing her too.

28

"And so, I told the shop assistant, if she did not know the origin of avocado, she did not deserve to have employment in a shop like that," Beverley finished her sixth glass of wine. "I mean, this was Waitrose. You expect better. I told her manager she would be better suited at Asda."

"My mother," Chloe leaned closer to me, whispering. "She acts like a great work coach for the elite but has never worked a bloody day in her life."

I had to laugh. It was day five of our holiday, and the night Miranda had asked us to join them all for a meal. I'm glad I did. I was feeling awkward around Zack, wondering whether I should bring up my issues with Chloe. It didn't feel right. They have known each other for a long time. Longer than I have known him. I have always fought on the side of men and women being friends, without it meaning anything. I have always managed it, but this one was bothering me. But if I brought it up, would it cause an argument? I didn't want a fall out with him as well as my best friend. That was too much emotion to handle. I don't think any of this would have even bothered me before my conversation with Sarah about the threat of the twenty-somethings. I know she was bitter at the time, going through that awful breakup herself, but maybe some part of her theory stuck with me, and that was why I was being weary. Should I feel threatened by Chloe?

She was a completely different person tonight. Very little flesh on show, although Zack had told me that her parents are conservative, so it was probably for their benefit that she was covered up this evening. She was quite reserved, only sipping her wine, and spent most of the dinner talking to me.

"Zack told me all about your cat," she said. "I'd love a pet, but Daddy is allergic. Did he really leave a dead mouse in your toilet?"

"Oh yes, it wasn't much fun fishing that out of the bowl. He likes to leave me treats every now and then. Particularly spiders in my shoes."

We laughed together, like we were besties on a night out. Her parents were snobs, but she was the complete opposite, and we sniggered like schoolgirls every time her mother shared another first world problem. She was actually being really friendly. I felt like such a hypocrite, so I decided to stop being such a knob. She is young and probably doesn't understand the concept of boundaries with guys. I know I didn't care at that age, so why should she?

"And they ran out of hummus!" Beverley's voice soon overpowered the table. "This is the twenty-first century. How can there be a hummus shortage?"

"It was probably my sister-in-law," I whispered to Zack. "Stocking up for winter."

He hid his laugh behind his bottle of Becks, longing, like the rest of us, for this night to come to an end.

"Well, Beverley, maybe you should start ordering online," Alistair piped up. He had been quiet all night, but not out of choice. Once Beverley started complaining about trivial matters, she couldn't stop.

"Pfft, online, have you heard him?" She nudged Miranda with her hand. "Mr Techno. Once you put in your bank account details, they take all your money. Those, those, what are they called? Trackers?"

"Hackers," Alistair corrected her.

"Yes, hackers. They take it all and leave you with cookies!"

"Cookies? What are you on about mother?"

"Cookies, haven't you heard of them? That Martin Lewis talked about it on *This Morning*. They do some peculiar things these technical thieves. They leave cookies on your computer, or something like that."

I could see Zack resisting the urge to correct her, deciding it was much more fun to let her go on.

"What do you kids have planned for the rest of this week then?" Miranda asked us, desperate to change the conversation. "I hope you'll find time to come shopping with me, Jenny. Zack mentioned you loved all the little shops in town. Men don't appreciate shopping like us."

"I'd love to, that would be great."

"We could go tomorrow, do you have plans?"

"No, I don't think so." I looked at Zack who shook his head.

"Great, we can go after breakfast," Miranda smiled.

"I want to take Jenny to Spinalonga at some point," Zack said. "She can't come to Crete without a bit of local history. I was going to try book tickets online but Beverley has me worried I'll be attacked by the Cookie monster."

The table erupted with laughter and Chloe spat her wine across the table.

"Chloe!" Beverley snapped. "Clean this up immediately, you're an embarrassment." She used her napkin to wipe her own arms, whilst the smile disappeared from Chloe's face.

"I didn't mean to, I had a mouthful of wine and Zack made me laugh."

"You two are always messing about, one way or another. At least he has settled down with a nice girl, what are you doing with yourself these days?"

"Beverley…" Stan tried to calm his wife, but it didn't work.

"Galivanting here and there, ringing your dad for money because you've lost your bank card off some ravine in the remote islands of wherever. It's about time you sorted yourself out. Get your law degree and grow up!"

I looked at Chloe whose face was now beetroot. She was furious. I felt such sympathy for this girl who, up until now, I had started to hate, when really, she and I had a lot in common. I thought of my own mother, who often spoke down to me when I was that age. As I got older, I learned to take it with a pinch of salt, with the occasional sarcastic reply or not replying to her messages. My mother wanted me to study business at university, but I chose English instead. Had I not chosen that subject, I never would have met Sarah.

Finally, the grown ups took their leave from the table, leaving us kids in an awkward silence.

"Sorry about my mum," Chloe said. "She gets a serious case of Bitchitus when she's had too much to drink."

"Are you alright?" Zack asked her.

"Yeah, of course. Excuse me for a moment, will you?" she stood up and made her way inside.

"Oh my god," I whispered to Zack. "That dinner took a mighty turn very quickly."

"Beverley can get like that, I think my mum hoped having you here would calm her down a bit. Beverley is great when she's sober, but once she's had a drink, you can bet money she will pick on Chloe one way or another. The thing is, she doesn't even know what's going on."

"What do you mean?"

"Chloe did go back to uni, but not to study law. She's doing a journalism degree. She comes across as immature, but she has a good head on her shoulders. Her dad knows and sends her money every now and then. She graduates next month."

"Why hasn't she told her mum?"

"Because," I looked up as Chloe reappeared at the table. "I'm going to get my first-class honours, start my job with Marie Claire and my mother can suck it." She placed a bottle of ouzo on the table. "Anyone up for some of this?"

I really wasn't, I had wanted an early night with Zack, but I didn't want to be the boring old fart.

"Maybe a couple," Zack said. "I'm shattered."

Zack and I went for a long walk on the beach this morning. We paddled, cooling our feet in the sea, before enjoying lunch in a small, family run café. The beach was filled with loved up couples, not a child in sight. The benefit of going on holiday during term time.

"I'll be back in a minute," I said. "I just want to top up on after sun. My shoulders are tingling a bit."

"Do you want a hand?" Zack tugged on my arm playfully, pulling me down for a kiss.

"I'll be fine, you two get started on the shots."

I had left the after sun in our bathroom after I'd had a shower. Zack smothered me in the stuff, hoping for some afternoon delight, but I had been feeling far too badly burned for bodily contact at that moment.

Up in the bathroom, I found the bottle and carefully rubbed it into my shoulders, which felt as though they had been slapped repeatedly. Borrowing Chloe's factor ten was a mistake. I will be back on the thirty tomorrow.

I heard music playing from outside, so I had a peak out of the bathroom window. Zack and Chloe were sat together on a sun lounger. He was whispering in her ear, a big smile on her face appeared before she flung out her arms and hugged him, pushing him so hard they ended up laid back on the seat with her on top of him.

I felt sick.

I was going to throw up.

What had he said to her to make her so giddy? Why did she feel the need to throw herself at him and lie on top of him? Are they both insane? What are they trying to do to me?

I had to do it.

"Hello?" It took a while for her to speak when she answered the phone, but Sarah's voice sounded uncertain.

"Hi." Unable to hide my emotion, I cried down the phone. "I need to talk to someone."

"What's happened? Are you alright?"

"It's Zack, I don't know what's going on. One minute we're all loved up and it's great," I stopped to take a breath, "but there's this girl here. This family friend, twenty-something, super hot, sexy girl and she's all over him. I thought it was just her, but he doesn't do anything to stop it. And just now, from the upstairs window, I just watched them all over each other in a private conversation, then she ended up on top of him."

"She what?! How could he do that to you?" she was furious.

"I don't know. I figured she was just an attention seeking whore-bag, but he's loving it. And she is ALWAYS there. We went for a lunch in town, she was there. We had some naughty pool antics, she was watching. We had a pool day just us, she was there. And now, after she's practically been my best friend all night, she's all over my boyfriend. I don't know what to do."

"Have you spoke to him? Found out what's going on? You need to tell Zack that you're upset." I had missed her voice.

"I will, tomorrow. I think I'm just going to go to bed for now. I'm out with his mum tomorrow, so tomorrow evening I can chat to him, once I've had a few hours away to think about things."

There was silence between us.

"How's Bing doing?"

"He attacked and successfully killed my laundry basket today. And now I'm missing a bra."

"Glad to hear he's settled in quickly."

29

"You were up early. How are you feeling this morning?" Zack joined me at the breakfast counter where I was picking at a croissant. "Have you still got a migraine?" He put his arm around me and kissed me on the head.

"No, it's not too bad this morning, I'm glad I avoided the ouzo though. Did you, erm, have a fun night?"

"Yeah, Chloe is mental. I'm too old for shots now though. I feel like such an old man next to her." He helped himself to coffee. "Is it too much sun, do you think? With your headache? Your shoulders looked pretty burned yesterday, maybe the walk on the beach was a bad idea. And there was me trying to be romantic, ha."

I tried to laugh with him, but it wasn't convincing.

"What are you getting up to this morning whilst I'm out with your mum?"

"Not much, probably chill with my dad." There was no mention of Chloe, which was a relief. "Are you sure you're alright?" He joined me at counter, pulling out the stool next to me. "If you're not feeling up to it, my mum won't mind. She won't be offended if you just want to hang out here for the day. There's plenty of time to shop, we've got another full week here yet."

"I'm fine, honestly don't worry."

He pulled my face towards his and placed a kiss on my non-responsive lips.

"You'd tell me though, right? If something was wrong, if something was bothering you?"

"Of course, it's all good. I think the migraine last night took it out of me. I just need some retail therapy and I'll be fine this afternoon."

"Are you sure?"

"Yeah, I'm sure."

"Good morning campers!" Miranda entered the kitchen. In her white shorts, blue blouse and straw hat, she was ready for a girl's day out. "Zack, don't let your father sit inside watching the tele with Stan all day. He needs some vitamin D. Make sure he sits outside for a while."

"Will do, mum."

"Are you alright Jenny? You look quite pale."

"She wasn't too good last night, are you sure you're up for it today?" Zack looked worried.

"I promise I'm ok," I stood up, brushing the crumbs from my hand onto my plate. "It was a rough night but a girly day is what the doctor ordered."

"I'm glad to hear it." And she genuinely looked happy to be heading out with me. I guess with having only a son, she missed out on these girly things. I only wish I could guarantee there would be more in the future. It depends on how my chat with Zack goes, I guess.

Miranda had called for a taxi.

"I thought we were going to Elounda?" I asked as we took the short trip to Agios Nikolaos.

"Oh, I changed my mind, is that alright? There are more shops here, so I thought it'd be more fun."

"That's fine." I could finally look in all the little shops and spend some money. That would take my mind off things. "I love looking at all the handmade jewellery."

"Well, let's see what we can buy and fill up our suitcases. We have all day. Zack will be busy getting things ready."

"Ready for what?"

"Oh didn't he tell you? He's useless sometimes, that boy. Must be a man thing," she laughed, shaking her head. "It's our thirty fifth wedding anniversary today."

"Oh wow, congratulations!" I beamed.

"Yes, we thought we'd have a special dinner tonight." My stomach flipped. Another dinner with Beverley the drunken witch and Chloe her trampy daughter and the husband who sits quietly and lets it all happen. Just what I needed. "It'll only be the four of us, so a little bit more intimate."

Phew.

"That sounds lovely. Well, if it is a special occasion, we have a lot of shopping to do."

We got out of the taxi and linked arms as we set off on our trip. It was already lifting me out of my mood, and once again, I was doubting myself. Was Zack really being that inappropriate? Was it all only one sided? Am I getting myself paranoid because I have finally found a guy I love and want to spend my life with and am worried I am going to lose him to a tramp whore, just like my best friend did?

Two hours into shopping, I had bought myself some gorgeous Greek jewellery, a mini statue of a minotaur, a new handheld fan (which I couldn't wait to show Zack) and I even got Sarah a little gift too. Even if our relationship was on the rocks, she has been looking after my cat. And if I know Bing… he will be keeping her on her toes.

"I just want to go back in that boutique before we eat, is that alright?" Miranda asked.

"Of course, go ahead. I'll wait outside."

"Ok, I'll be two minutes, I might buy that dress after all."

I watched as she went in and was welcomed back by the shop assistant who spoke perfect English. I pulled out my phone. There was no message from Sarah, so I decided on a browse on Facebook. Curiosity got the better of me, so I searched for my new favourite twenty-something.

Her profile was public, so I could browse what Chloe had been up to. We had our mutual friend, my boyfriend, and she had tagged herself as on holiday in Crete. The status updates were cringey, I wonder if Marie Claire had seen her use of the English language.

"OMG wel annoyd, mum driving me up the waaaaalll!!!"

"Gr8ful for old m8s xx"

"Nothing lyk a cuddl from Z to make thngs better X"

"Big plans...cant w8!!!"

'Z'? Zack? And what are her big plans? Do they include Zack?

Oh, another status has been posted...

"Day out with Z, exciting things 2 come x"

What the... is he spending the day with her? Where are they? What are they doing? Why wouldn't he tell me? Why did he even bring me here if he was just wanting to spend the day with her?

I was fuming. I pulled out my new fan and flapped at my face to try cool myself down. I didn't know whether I wanted to scream or cry.

And then I saw them.

There they were, linking arms, walking down the road, totally oblivious. But, of course, they thought we were going to Elounda. They could be free from being discovered here. No old girlfriend, no judgey parents, they could do what they liked.

I watched from behind my fan as they walked into one of the boutiques. Zack held the door open for her, he was always such a gentleman.

Pulling my phone out, I wanted to call him, but instinct sent me somewhere else.

"It's over," I typed in a message to Sarah. "He's with her now. I'm with his mum, shopping."

She replied instantly.

"OMG! Wanker! Can I call you?"

"No, if I talk about it, I'll cry. Can you see if there are any flights out for me tonight?"

"I'll have a look, but please TALK to him tonight. He has no idea you're feeling like this. Promise me you'll talk to him. Then call me and we'll see if you still want a flight home xx"

I agreed to hold off on making a dramatic exit until I spoke to him. I would wait until after the anniversary dinner so I wouldn't ruin the night. But my heart was breaking. Celebrating a wedding anniversary was the last thing I needed right now.

We were all seated around the table. Alistair had just cooked us a wonderful dinner, something I had never even thought of trying before, barbequed lobster. My sister-in-law would have had a stroke had she witnessed the carnage, but it was delicious.

The food was great, but the tension at the table reeked of rotten fish. I was obviously quiet given my devastating discovery, but Zack seemed to be acting funny too. Guilt, maybe? When we got back from shopping, I had asked about his day, and he stuttered that he had been relaxing by the pool for most of it, reading a book. The lie cut right through my gut.

I just had to keep calm and cool until later on tonight. Once Miranda and Alistair go to bed, I will talk to him and find out what has been going on and, the dreaded question, has he been having an affair with Chloe.

"I'd like to make a toast." Zack stood up and his parents smiled.

Alistair topped up everyone's glasses with wine and put his arm around Miranda who snuggled in close to him. They looked so happy, even after thirty five years of marriage.

I never thought Zack would be the type to make a speech, and judging by how much his upper lip was sweating, he mustn't do this very often.

"Mum, Dad, I'd like to wish you a very happy anniversary. You have been a huge inspiration, not only as parents but as a couple. It is by your example which leads me to what I am about to do." I could see a tear in his mum's eye. He turned to me. "Jenny, I know I've been acting weird today, and maybe the last few days, but see, I had a plan."

His hands were shaking. "This last year has been the best, most exciting and enjoyable time of my life. I have fallen deep in love, I cannot imagine my life without you. So, Jenny," he put down his glass and pulled a small box out of his pocket. Pushing back his chair, he got down on one knee in front of me and said… "will you marry me?"

30

I felt like I had been thumped in the chest. I couldn't breathe. There was no air.

"Jenny?" I think Zack said my name, but I can't be sure. "Jenny, are you alright?"

"I th…" I opened my mouth, but could hardly form any words. "I thought… you and… I need some water."

"Ali, why don't we give these two a moment." Miranda could sense something was wrong, clearly our new mother and daughter bond was stronger than I realised.

"Are you alright?" Zack was still on his knees in front of me, the box now open and a beautiful, white gold ring with a diamond studded band with a square cut diamond in the centre was looking up at me.

"I thought you and Chloe…"

"Me and Chloe? What about us?"

"I saw you. Last night, she was on top of you, and you've been so close. And then today I saw you in town with her but you lied, and…" I was so short of breath by now, my nose all stuffed from snot and tears wasn't helping. "I thought you were cheating on me." I finally said it as I started to cry properly.

"I would never do that to you!" He was crying now too. "Is that what you thought? I'm so sorry, but, I should probably have said from the beginning… I didn't even think…"

"What?"

What was he going to tell me? Did they have a history? Did they sleep together last year but decide to stay friends? Were they friends with benefits before I came along?

"Chloe is gay."

"She… she's what?"

"She's gay," he was whispering now. "She is dating a girl back home. They've been on the same course for three years and living together for two. She's been keeping it from her Mum."

"She's gay? But you were so, close."

"She's like my little sister, of course we're close. And I am so sorry you thought something else, I'm mortified." He wiped his eyes with his napkin. "She will be too. She'll say, 'oh ma gaaad that's so gross' and pretend to vomit."

I couldn't help but laugh at his impression.

"But today, you lied. You were with her, and said you were here."

"Jenny, look at this box." He shut the ring box and I saw the name, Devarakis. It was a jewellery shop in the local town. "I had ordered the ring a few weeks ago, with the help of Chloe who was already here. She went to collect it with me."

I thought back to her Facebook update, *"Day out with Z, exciting things 2 come x"*.

"You planned to propose all this time?"

"Yes, I wanted to be traditional, but with your Dad not being here, I called your brother."

Andrew. That is why he was at my house.

"You asked Andrew for permission to marry me?" the tears were back, but they weren't angry tears. They weren't even sad tears.

"Yes, I called him and when I said you weren't in, he wanted to come over. He drove over especially. We had a nice chat, and I promised at the wedding to slip some cocktail sausages into his tofu."

I laughed, a much needed laugh. My body relaxed as he laughed with me, holding my hands.

"So, Jenny," he wiped his eyes, and whilst still on one knee, he reopened the small box. "Will you marry me?"

31

I pulled up outside Sarah's house, ready to collect Bing and see how much compensation Sarah wanted for damages to her new home. As long as he hasn't touched her sofa, I think we can get away with it.

Sarah and I hadn't spoken since my mini meltdown in Agios Nikolaos. She text me every day, asking if I was alright, but I never gave anything away.

"Hey," she tried to smile as she opened the door, but she was nervous. As she stepped to one side, I went in. There was no clear damage that I could see. Bing hadn't clawed at any of the walls. "Shall I put the kettle on?"

"I think you should. I, erm, I'm ready to talk about, about you and Dan."

"Ok," she exhaled. She had clearly been expecting this, and had a speech prepared. "I am so, so, so, so sorry. Dan and I weren't meant to happen. I arranged a date with a guy from the app, he didn't show up, but Dan was there. We had a drink, we had a laugh, we decided to have our own date," she stopped for a much needed breath. "We really hit it off. We spoke on the phone. We texted. We went out again. I just," her hand covered her mouth to stop her lip from quivering. "If I'd known," her voice went high. "If I'd known it would cause this, between us, I never would have…" that was it. She was gone.

I hugged my crying friend.

"It's ok."

"No, it isn't." she pulled back. "I kept it from you. You and I don't keep things. It was really shitty of me. I don't know why I kept it from you. It was stupid!"

"Sarah, look, it was a big thing. I get it. I was hurt you couldn't talk to me. But not speaking to you for two weeks has hurt me even more. I need you."

"Well, I spoke to Dan about it all and we might be calling it off."

"What on earth for?"

"I told him my friendship was more important. We've been together since we were eighteen. We've seen it all with each other. And after Max The Wanker, you pulled me back to life."

That was it. We were both crying now. We hugged and soaked each other's shoulders with tears that had been a long time coming. But I was not losing my friend over a guy, and she was not losing a guy over me.

"Sarah, you're not going to stop seeing him, do you hear me?" I pulled back and held on to her shoulders. Her blond hair was stained dark from the tears. "Do you like him? I mean, really like him?"

"I do."

"Then there you go. We can all be happy now. Ok?"

"I don't want things to be awkward though, I mean, you and he…"

"All history. All forgotten. So, are we having that cuppa or what?"

My friend laughed and switched the kettle on. I felt something familiar on my leg.

"Oh, hello you. You finally come to say hello." I stroked Bing's head who was chuntering under his breath, his own way of saying, 'where the hell have you been?' "Shall we get your stuff together?"

"I'll bring the drinks to the room," Sarah said. "Go get comfy."

"When are you seeing Dan next then?" I asked as she handed me my cuppa.

"I'll text him in a bit. I think he's expecting me to call it off so it'll hopefully be a nice surprise when I say otherwise."

"Yes, it will. I'm so glad you've found someone. Before I went away, you seemed happier. I thought it was because you were getting rid of me for a while but I guess there was another reason."

"I haven't felt this happy in ages. When he texts me, I get all smiley and giddy. And, that day you found us, that was the first time we, you know."

"Ohh, I was witness to a milestone!" I laughed. "I'm glad I can be part of that memory."

"Jenny, honestly, if this is going to be weird, I will end things with him."

"You're not going to end things with him. You're going to need him around in about twelve months time."

"Why's that?"

"You'll need a date. Oh, didn't I tell you?"

"Tell me what?" The anticipation was killing her.

"I didn't tell you? I can't believe it slipped my mind." With my left hand, I rubbed my forehead in shame. How could I forget to tell her?

"Wait," she said. "Is that? Are you...?"

"Oh this?" I held out my left hand, clearly displaying the most beautiful engagement ring in the history of jewellery. "Yeah, Zack gave it to me in exchange for promising to be his wife."

"Ahhhh!" our tea spilled all over her new couch as she launched herself at me, hugging me. She examined the ring as I told her everything that had happened on the night of the anniversary dinner. How Zack and I cried as we opened up. The things he said as he asked me to marry him. How his mum cried and hugged us whilst Alistair popped open a bottle of champagne. How Chloe had been watching from her window and crying at how happy her 'big bro' was and how thrilled she was that I was going to be her big sister.

"I've already asked her to be a bridesmaid, but I have a bigger role for you." I pulled a small bag from my pocket and handed it to Sarah, watching her pull out a handmade bracelet of silver with green gems. "Will you be my maid of honour?"

"Jenny," her voice broke. "I would love to be your maid of honour." Our next hug was a more mature and loving embrace. We held on tight for what felt like ages, glad to be back in each other's lives.

A text from Zack two hours later interrupted our much needed catch up.

"How's it all going? Xxx"

"All good in the hood, won't be long, love you Xxx"

"Take your time, have fun Xxx"

"So, we have so much to plan!" Sarah bounced up from the couch, retrieving a notepad and pen from the kitchen. "We need wedding dress shops, florists, venues, photographers… I'm pretty sure a few of those would offer me a discount with the amount of money they had from me for nothing in return. I can call them if you like? Oh, and the most important thing of all!"

"What's that?"

"The hen do!"

"Don't plan anything huge, I'm an old woman now. Just something sensible close to home. No naked men serving onion rings on their penises."

"Nah, I know what we're doing for your hen do. And it is perfect."

"What?"

"Zante."

This renewed friendship might not last very long.

From the author

I hope you enjoyed reading 'Holiday Date' as much as I enjoyed writing it and bringing the characters back for a second round of antics.

Read on for a BONUS extra chapter ;)

Zante 2010

I pulled Sarah's groping hands out of my bikini top.

"Will you stop! Everyone will think we're lesbians!" The resort was quite busy at that moment.

"That's not a bad thing," Sarah observed our mainly male audience who were eyeing her up. "Look at them all. Soak it all up while you can." She whipped her hair behind her shoulders and leaned back in her chair, feet up on her suitcase. "Anyway, I'm just trying to give you a little more cleavage, pull them up yourself. You've got great boobs. Show 'em off."

"I don't see why we had to put our bikinis on right now, we haven't even been given our room key yet." I felt very self-conscious sitting in such a public place in a bikini top. Sarah had let me keep my shorts on, for now. It wouldn't be long until she was insisting my pasty white legs were out in the sun too.

Our rep was being held hostage by an angry couple at the hotel entrance, so had told us all to wait in the outdoor dining area. Sarah comfortably sat back in her chair, whereas I was using my bag to hide my belly. This was not a flattering position.

"Fancy a dip in the pool? We can really drive them wild."

"No, I don't!"

"Come on Jenny, you promised you'd loosen up on this trip. Live a little. We're twenty-one! Uni is done, this is the start of our last summer of freedom. Start to relax."

"I will, I will, just not yet. I want to unpack and figure out where I'm sleeping tonight. Get my bearings."

"It'll be fine, we're up there somewhere." She pointed to the rooms looking over us. "Just relax."

Celeste Apartments was like a miniature village. The pool took centre stage, surrounded by sun loungers and small tables. There was a bar and a shop on one side, and a restaurant on the other, with four floors of apartments in between. The whole place was surrounded by a white concrete wall, which made me feel very secure. I've never been on holiday without my parents before. I could always rely on Dad to have his watchful eye over me, but he can't do that all the way from Halifax. I am at the mercy of my horny friend Sarah who was lapping the attention.

"Hiya guys!" our very animated Scouser rep, Gaz, appeared with his clipboard in his right hand, and his left hung in the air as though he was holding on to an invisible cigarette. "Riiight, so sorry about the delay, oof, it warm innit? Ok, I see you ladies couldn't wait to get started on the tan." He winked at us. "So, we're just about ready now. If you make your way to reception, we can get started."

"Finally," I was getting hungry. It was nearly five o'clock. We'd not eaten since our pre-flight Burger King from Manchester Airport this morning.

"Right, I say we dump our bags and come straight back down. Get some pool action before the sun disappears." Sarah insisted.

"Well…"

"I know you want to unpack, but we can do that later. It looks like the bar serves light snacks and brings them to you while you're sunbathing. We can have a light bite now and eat properly later."

"I guess we could."

"Yes, we can. You look so good in that bikini."

"I don't feel it," I blushed. "I'm just not used to this."

"I know, but I promise, you look fab. How do I look?"

"Absolutely stunning."

"Aw thanks babes." She bounced forward, kissing me on the cheek. "Come on, let's get in the queue for our room."

There was no messing around. As soon as we had our keys, we were up to the second floor looking for our room. Sarah found it in no time. I didn't even get a foot in the door before Sarah pulled my suitcase from me and shoved it inside, quickly locking the door again.

"Can't we look around?"

"Yes, later, come on, let's get back down to the pool! I spotted some free sun loungers. I wonder if those lads are still there."

They were. There were four lads accompanied by two lasses. The girls were coupled up with two of the guys, leaving two singletons who were very interested in us. In between swigging their beers and puffing on cigarettes, they kept looking our way, trying to catch our eyes.

"So, we need a plan of action," Sarah sipped on her cocktail and turned to face me on her sun lounger. "We're only here for a week, we need to make the most of it."

"I'm sure the rep could give us some idea of day trips."

"No, not day trips, you spoon. I'm talking about fun. We just worked our arses off for our exams, and we're about to enter the exciting world of adulthood. This is our last chance to go wild!"

My cocktail was beginning to settle in my empty stomach, and I could already feel it hitting me. I suddenly felt the need to dance.

"We need to find some kind of dance club or something," I suggested.

"Yes!" she held out her glass and loudly called out. "Girls on tour!"

"Woo, girls on tour!"

"Girls on tour!" we said in unison.

We clinked glasses and giggled as both of our eye candies held up their drinks to us and cheered. It was true, we had worked bloody hard over the last few months. I'd barely seen Sarah, even though we had been living together in our own very tiny student flat. She might be my crazy best friend, but once she gets her study head on, she is unapproachable. That's if you can find her. However, once the pressure is off, she more than makes up for it.

As the sun went down, the lights around the pool came on and guided us back to the stairs, helping us to avoid falling into the water. Balance was becoming an issue.

"Come on," Sarah said, "we can have a quick shower, freshen up and then try the restaurant. Have some food, refuel, then head out. What do you think?"

"Sounds like a plan." I gripped the bannister, laughing at myself as I almost tripped on the second step. "I thought they were supposed to water down the drinks here, mine were really strong."

"Mine too, we've barely eaten though. A splash of cold water and we'll be… oh, hello."

I looked up to see the two singletons alongside us.

"Hello," his accent was instantly recognisable. "Where are you girls from?"

"Yorkshire," I answered, trying to keep my eyes on him. Although I was finding it difficult to focus properly, I could just make out his green eyes. They pulled me in, like

Kaa from the *Jungle Book*. However, apart from a slithery snake, it was a very fit Essex boy.

"Oh, I love Yorkshire," he smiled.

"Is that right?" I laughed. "And if we were from Newcastle, I bet you'd love that too."

"Absolutely."

"Ignore my friend," Sarah said. "She's not into cheesy chat up lines."

"Oh yeah? How about you?" asked Essex number two.

"You can try me." She twirled her hair between her fingers, looking up at him.

"Well, how about this." He put his hands on his hips, accepting the challenge. "Your blonde hair is beautiful, is it natural?"

"No," she said quickly, "it's supernatural. Don't upset me or it might curse you."

"Ha!" Both Essex boys laughed. "I'm Taz," said Sarah's daring love interest, "this is my pal Joe. Aren't you girls sticking around for the party?"

"What party?" Sarah asked.

"The hotel is throwing a big bash tonight, big pool party. It's gonna be mint. Kicks off in a few minutes. Are you coming back down?"

"We might be, we could be convinced." Sarah winked at me.

"We'll see you back down there then, I hope."

I blushed as Joe gave me one last smile before heading back down to their spot by the pool.

"Oh my God, Sarah!" I said when they were out of ear shot. "They were fit as. What are we wearing tonight? Will you do my make up? Are we going to the party?"

"Of course we're going," she hooked her arm around mine and led me back down the stairs. "But we don't need to get changed. It's a pool party, we're fine as we are. Come on."

A few hours later, we were still sat around the pool with our Essex boys, and things were progressing very quickly. Cocktail after cocktail was being consumed, and the more I drank, the more X-rated the situation was becoming. The boys had told us they were leaving tomorrow, which spurred us on to make the night even more exciting.

"Why don't we move the party upstairs?" I heard Taz suggest to Sarah.

"Yeah, your room?" Sarah asked.

"We can't, it's shared with the others. How about yours?"

"We could do, hey, Jenny?"

"Yeah?"

"We're going up, private party. You guys coming?"

I looked at Joe, he smelled great. I have never had a one-night stand, ever, but he was too good to let go. Essex is a million miles away, so it's not like I can hop on the bus to visit him. It was now or never.

"How about it?" I asked, fearful he would turn me down, even now.

"Yeah, if you're sure. What's your place like? Do you have separate rooms?"

"Erm, I don't know." I still hadn't seen the bedroom as Sarah hadn't let me inside. "I think it's one bedroom, but there's a balcony we can chill on, although I'm not sure if there's any furniture." It was still warm outside, so no reason we couldn't sit out.

"Well, we can find out?" Joe reached for my hand and pulled me up so we could follow Sarah and Taz up to our room. I was glad Joe had hold of me. Drinking on an empty stomach almost resulted in a midnight dip in the pool.

"Here we are!" Sarah opened the door to our room and I could finally have a look around, although there wasn't much to look at.

"Sarah, didn't you request separate beds?" It's a good thing Sarah and I are such good friends as we're about to get very close for the next seven nights. I peeked my head in the door to my right, finding a shower room with a sink and toilet. Not even a bath to chill out in. There were no other rooms, this was it. A queen-sized bed and a small two-seater sofa.

Joe walked around the bed and opened up the balcony doors.

"Your balcony isn't a bad size, could pull the couch out here."

I joined him by the double doors, I didn't want to upset the managers by moving furniture around. One glance behind me at Sarah and Taz smooching on the bed quickly changed my mind though. Joe and I managed to pull the couch out and closed the door behind us, leaving Sarah and Taz to it.

"We'll leave them alone for a while I think." Joe seemed embarrassed by his friend, or perhaps gutted that he didn't get the bed first. "So, nice view."

I looked out to the darkness. I could hear the sea, but have no idea where it was, or what was facing our room. I'm guessing nothing, since there are no lights beside the one shining down on us.

"Shall we," I hesitated. "Do you want to sit down?"

"It'd be rude not to, seeing as I made you drag it out here with me." He laughed as we sat down together. I suddenly had butterflies in my tummy. I felt like a fifteen-year-old girl about to kiss her first boy. Sarah was right, I am frigid, but only with boys that I like. I hope I grow out of this eventually. I'll make sure that I do.

"So, erm, what time are you off tomorrow?" I was struggling to find something interesting to talk about. The more he looked into my eyes, the more I panicked. Has my make up smudged? Do I look fat? Do I smell?

"Early," he said, looking down at my lips, getting closer.

"So, you'll erm, be wanting an early night…"

"Yeah, I probably should…"

As soon as his lips met mine, there was no stopping us. Clothes, the small amount we had on, were pulled off. Things moved fast, alcohol a big factor in this decision. That tiny soberness still inside me made sure he had a condom, which he pulled out of his pocket and put on whilst I glanced out into the darkness on the other side of the railings.

This was it. My first one night stand. Popping my Zante cherry.

We found ourselves competing with the noises coming from inside, not caring that there were rooms on either side of us, or lights shining down on us. After a few surprisingly satisfying minutes, we fell asleep together, still interlocked and naked.

Tap tap.

Taz's knocking on the glass door woke us up. Sober, and cold, I used Joe's shirt to cover up. The sky was orange, but I couldn't focus on anything, the dim light hurting my sensitive eyes. A holiday hangover was not intended so soon.

"Mate, we gotta go. Coach'll be here soon," Taz said as he slid the door open.

"Comin' mate." Joe rubbed his eyes and put his clothes on. I stepped inside, picking up a neatly rolled towel which had fallen to the floor and wrapped it around me, handing Joe his shirt back. "It was nice meeting you," he said, giving me a quick kiss.

I allowed him to kiss me, the shame seeping out of my pores along with the vodka I'd consumed last night. I didn't want to look at him. I just wanted to climb into bed. Once the balcony and room doors were closed, and both guys had left, I climbed into bed and joined Sarah in a long, dehydrated, hungover sleep.

Bang, bang.

Either my head was about to implode, or someone was at the door. I hoped it was the latter.

"Jenny…" Sarah's weak voice called out. "Jenny, the door."

"I know."

Bang, Bang.

"Hang on," she called to the impatient visitors whilst struggling to sit herself up. "Goddam cleaners."

"Not today!" I shouted at the door.

"Can ya let me in?" Gaz's unmistakable voice called through the door. "We need to talk."

"What does he want?" I asked.

"Hopefully telling us we were given the wrong room." She threw back the bed sheet and threw on her kaftan. "I'm coming."

I readjusted my towel to make sure I was covered when Gaz walked in, accompanied by a man in a suit, making me quickly jump out of bed.

"What's going on?" Sarah asked.

"This is the hotel manager. It seems, erm, there was a complaint made to the hotel this morning." Gaz spoke with a serious tone, but something about his lips hinted he wanted to laugh. "Was someone out on the balcony last night?"

I could feel my face burning up as Gaz and the manager walked to the sliding doors.

"Erm, well…" I looked at Sarah, who was almost blushing too.

"Well, I have a complaint of my own." She crossed her arms and looked at the manager. "We have been given the wrong room. I specifically booked a twin room with a separate living area. This is just ridiculous. No wonder one of us was forced to sleep outside."

"Well, from the nature of the complaint, there wasn't much sleeping going on." Gaz's eyes looked at mine and then eyed something on the floor of the balcony. It was the used condom. I wanted to die on the spot. The manager took one look at the condom, nodded at Gaz and then stomped out of the room. As soon as the manager was gone… "I'm so sorry girls, but you have to leave."

"Eh!" We said together.

"Do you see the house opposite yours? That *massive* villa?"

"Yeah," I said, seeing the view for the first time. The villa was barely five meters from our room, and it was huge.

"You put on quite a show last night for the visiting Prince Abdulla of Saudi Arabia and his three sons. They're about to declare war!"

"What! You're pulling my leg, seriously, there's no way…"

Gaz pulled out his phone. "My manager's calling, hang on. Hello? Yeah, yeah. I'm with them now, yeah. Alright. No, no, no police. No. No! Yeah. Yeah. Alright. Yeah. Fab, mate. That's fab. I'll tell them."

"Police?" I could feel the colour draining from my face.

"No, they've had the Consulate dealing with it. It's fine. Well, it will be fine once we get you two outta here. Pack your things."

"Wait, is this going to be on the news?" Police or not, if this ended up on the news, I'd be done for.

"Luckily for you, no. It's being dealt with. Come on, get your things, I'll meet you at the bottom of the stairs. There's a taxi here to take you to the airport."

Gaz rushed out of the room, leaving Sarah and I staring at each other in disbelief.

"Is this real?" I asked. "Is this really happening?"

"I think so. Wow. We know how to party."

I heard noise from the balcony. I looked long enough to see a group of men all stood in a window in the villa shouting words I didn't understand and shaking their heads. How is this even happening?

I don't think I'll be planning a return trip to Zante.

Ever.

To learn more about Debbie and her books, follow her on Facebook: www.facebook.com/debbieioannaauthor

Please remember to leave a review on Amazon :)

Thank you

Printed in Great Britain
by Amazon